Praise for *The Handle* and Rich

"Richard Stark (the name that when he lets Parker off the lea efficiency. His bad guys are polished pros who think hard, move fast, and turn on a dime in moments of crisis."

—Marilyn Stasio, *New York Times Book Review*

"Stark was, and is, a pseudonym for Donald Westlake, a writer so inventive and wildly fecund that he had no option but to publish under other names. . . . It's excellent to have [his novels] readily available again—not so much masterpieces of genre, just masterpieces, period."

—Richard Rayner, *Los Angeles Times*

"Richard Stark's Parker . . . is refreshingly amoral, a thief who always gets away with the swag."

—Stephen King, *Entertainment Weekly*

"The caper novel, the story of a major criminal operation from the point of view of the participants, has no better practitioner than Richard Stark."

—Anthony Boucher, *New York Times Book Review*

"Westlake's ability to construct an action story filled with unforeseen twists and quadruple-crosses is unparalleled."

—*San Francisco Chronicle*

The Handle

Parker Novels By Richard Stark

The Handle

RICHARD STARK

With a New Foreword by Luc Sante

The University of Chicago Press

The University of Chicago Press, Chicago 60637
© 1966 by Richard Stark
Foreword © 2009 by Luc Sante
All rights reserved.
University of Chicago Press edition 2009

Printed in the United States of America

18 17 16 15 14 13 12 11 10 09   1 2 3 4 5

ISBN-13: 978-0-226-77106-9 (paper)
ISBN-10: 0-226-77106-7 (paper)

Library of Congress Cataloging-in-Publication Data

Stark, Richard, 1933–2008.
  The handle / Richard Stark ; with a new foreword by Luc Sante.
     p. cm.
  ISBN-13: 978-0-226-77106-9 (alk. paper)
  ISBN-10: 0-226-77106-7 (alk. paper)
  1. Parker (Fictitious character) 2. Criminals—Fiction. I. Title.
PS3573.E9H3 2009
  813'.54—dc22
                              2009012977

Foreword

THE PARKER novels by Richard Stark are a singularly long-lasting literary franchise, established in 1962 and pursued to the present, albeit with a twenty-three-year hiatus in the middle. In other ways, too, they are a unique proposition. When I read my first Parker novel—picked up at random, and in French translation, no less—I was a teenager, and hadn't read much crime fiction beyond Sherlock Holmes and Agatha Christie. I was stunned by the book, by its power and economy and the fact that it blithely dispensed with moral judgment, and of course I wanted more. Not only did I want more Parker and more Stark, I also imagined that I had stumbled upon a particularly brilliant specimen of a thriving genre. But I was wrong. There is no such genre.

To be sure, there are plenty of tight, harsh crime novels, beginning with Dashiell Hammett's *Red Harvest,* and there is a substantial body of books written from the point of view of the criminal, ranging from the tortured cries of Jim Thompson and David Goodis to the mordantly analytical *romans durs* by Georges Simenon. There are quite a few caper novels, including the comic misadventures Parker's creator writes under his real name, Donald Westlake, and the works of a whole troop of French writers not well known in this country: José Giovanni, Albert Simonin, San-Antonio. The lean, efficient Giovanni in particular has points in common with Stark (Anglophones can best approach him through movie adaptations: Jean-Pierre Melville's *Le deuxième souffle,* Claude Sautet's *Classe tous risques*), but with the key difference that Giovanni is an unabashed romantic.

Stark is not a romantic, or at least not within the first six feet down from the surface. Westlake has said that he meant the books to be about "a workman at work," which they are, and that is why they have so few useful parallels, why they are virtually a genre unto themselves. Process and mechanics and troubleshooting dominate the books, determine their plots, underlie their aesthetics and their moral structure. A great many of the editions down through the years have prominently featured a blurb from Anthony Boucher: "Nobody tops Stark in his objective portrayal of a world of total amorality." That is true as far as it goes—it is never suggested in the novels that robbing payrolls or shooting people who present liabilities are anything more than business practices—but Boucher overlooked the fact that Parker maintains his own very lively set of moral prerogatives. Parker abhors waste, sloth, frivolity, inconstancy, double-dealing, and reckless endangerment as much as any Puritan. He hates dishonesty with a passion, although you and he may differ on its terms. He is a craftsman who takes pride in his work.

Parker is in fact a bit like the ideal author of a crime-fiction series: solid, dependable, attentive to every nuance and detail. He is annoyed by small talk and gets straight to the point in every instance, using no more than the necessary number of words to achieve his aim. He eschews shortcuts, although he can make difficult processes look easy, and he is free of any trace of sentiment, although he knows that while planning and method and structure are crucial, character is even more important. As brilliant as he is as a strategist, he is nothing short of phenomenal at instantly grasping character. This means that he sometimes sounds more like a fictional detective than a crook, but mostly he sounds like a writer. In order to decide which path the double-crosser he is pursuing is most likely to have taken, or which member of the string is most likely to double-cross, or the odds on a reasonable-sounding job that has just been proposed to him by someone with shaky credentials, he has to get all the way under the skin of the party in question. He is an exceptionally intelligent freelancer in a risky profession who takes on difficult jobs hoping for a payoff large enough to hold off the next job for as long as possible. He even has an agent (Joe Sheer succeeded by Handy McKay). Then again he is seen—by other characters as well as readers—as lacking in emotion, let alone sympathy, a thug whose sole motivation is self-interest.

And no wonder: Parker is a big, tough man with cold eyes. "His hands looked like they'd been molded of brown clay by a sculptor who thought big and liked veins"; the sentence appears like a Homeric epithet somewhere in an early chapter of most of the books. He might just possibly pass for a businessman, provided the business is something like used cars or jukeboxes. He doesn't drink much, doesn't gamble, doesn't read, likes to sit in the dark, thinking, or else in front of the television, not watching but employing it as an aid to concentration. Crude and antisocial at the start of the series, he actually evolves considerably over its course. Claire, whom he meets in *The Rare Coin Score,* seems to have a lot to do with this—by *Deadly Edge* they actually have a house together. And Alan Grofield, first encountered in *The Score* and recurring in *The Handle,* among other titles, twice in the series becomes the recipient of what can only be called acts of kindness from Parker, however much Stark equivocates on this point, insisting that they merely reflect professional ethics or some such.

Parker is a sort of supercriminal—not at all like those European master criminals, such as Fantômas and Dr. Mabuse, but a very American freebooter, able to outmaneuver the Mob, the CIA, and whatever other forces come at him. For all that he lives on the other side of the law, he bears a certain resemblance to popular avengers of the 1960s and '70s, Dirty Harry or Charles Bronson's character in *Death Wish*. He is a bit of a fanatic, and even though we are repeatedly told how sybaritic his off duty resort-hotel lifestyle is, it remains hard to picture, since he is such an ascetic in the course of the stories. He is so utterly consumed by the requirements of his profession that everything extraneous to it is suppressed when he's on, and we are not privy to his time off, except for narrow vignettes in which he is glimpsed having sex or, once, swimming. But then, writers are writing even when they're not writing, aren't they?

After *The Hunter*, all the remaining titles concern jobs gone wrong, which seems to be the case for most of Parker's jobs, barring the occasional fleeting allusion to smoother operations in the past. *The Seventh* is, naturally, the seventh book in the series, as well as a reference to the split from the take in a stadium job. The actual operation is successful; the problem is what occurs afterward. It represents the very rare incursion, for the Parker series, of a thriller staple: the crazed gunman. Along with *The Rare Coin Score*, it is one of Stark's always very-pointed explorations of group dynamics. *The Handle*, with its private gambling island, ex-Nazi villain, and international intrigue, is (like *The Mourner* and *The Black Ice Score*) a nod to the espionage craze of the 1960s, when authors of thrillers could not afford to ignore James Bond. If *The Seventh* is primarily aftermath, *The Handle* is largely preamble. In *The Rare Coin Score* (the first of four such titles, succeeded by *Green Eagle, Black Ice,* and *Sour Lemon*) the culprit is an amateur, a coin dealer whose arrested development is so convincingly depicted the reader can virtually hear his voice squeak. Sharp characterizations abound in this one—its plot turns entirely on character flaws of various sizes.

The Parker books are all engines, machines that start up with varying levels of difficulty, then run through a process until they are done, although subject to different sorts of interference. The heists depicted are only part of this process—sometimes they are even peripheral to it. Parker is the mechanic who runs the machine and attempts to keep it oiled and on course. The interference is always caused by personalities—by the greed, incompetence, treachery, duplicity, or insanity of individuals concerned, although this plays out in a variety of ways, depending on whether it affects the job at beginning, middle, or end, and whether it occurs as a single dramatic action, a domino sequence of contingencies, or a gradually fraying rope. The beauty of the machine is that not only does it allow for the usual suspense, but it also maximizes the effectiveness of its opposite: the satisfaction of inevitability. Some Parker novels are fantastically intricate clockwork mechanisms (*The Hunter, The Outfit,* the seemingly unstoppable *Slayground,* the epic *Butcher's Moon*), while others hurtle along as successions of breakdowns (the aptly acidic *The Sour Lemon Score,* the almost sadistically frustrating *Plunder Squad*). Like all machines but unlike lesser thrillers the novels have numerous moving parts, and the more the better—more people, more subplots, more businesslike detail, more glimpses of marginal lives. Stark's momentum is such that the more matter he throws into the hopper the faster the gears turn. The books are machines that all but read themselves. You can read the entire series and not once have to invest in a bookmark.

Luc Sante
December 2008

The Handle

ONE

1

When the engine stopped, Parker came up on deck for a look around. The mainland was nearly out of sight now, just a gray smudge on the horizon between the dark blue of the water and the lighter blue of the sky.

The man who called himself Yancy was sitting in one of the two chairs astern, and the man whose name Parker didn't know was standing at the controls. They both wore white trousers, navy blue jackets and yachting caps and sunglasses, but they both had the faces and voices and hands of New York or Chicago hoods.

Yancy raised the hand with the glass in it and motioned forward. "There it is," he said.

Parker turned and looked out past the spray-flecked windshield, over the top of the rest of the boat, and out over the water to the island. It was still about half a mile away, and all he could make out was a mound of jungle greenery bulging up out of the water over there.

"Get in closer," he said. "I can't see anything from here."

The one at the wheel said, "We don't want to take chances."

Yancy said, "He's right. Move in closer."

The guy at the wheel didn't like it, but he had nothing more to say. He just frowned behind his sunglasses, shrugged his shoulders, and started the engine.

Yancy waved the hand with the bottle in it. "Come on and sit down. Why stay below all the time?"

Parker had gone down into the cabin before they'd left the dock and had stayed there until just now. He had no fear of water, but he didn't like boats and he didn't like the ocean. Coming out away from land like this was like sticking yourself in a cage; there was no way out. From a practical point of view he was stuck on this boat, imprisoned on it, till it touched land again. So long as he stayed down below in the cabin, a place that looked like half the motel rooms in the southwest, he wasn't so aware of the caged feeling, but up here, surrounded by the flat blue water of the Gulf of Mexico, he was reminded of it all the time.

Still, the island was in sight, and that's what he'd come out here to see, so he went back and sat in the other white chair next to Yancy. The boat was pushing through the waves again, not very fast, heading toward the island.

Parker supposed it was a good boat, as boats go. It was an Owens cabin cruiser, forty feet long, sleek and gleaming, mostly white, with a blond wood deck. There were three rooms below, plus two baths, and space enough with convertible sofa and hideaway bed to sleep eight. The area up here where he and Yancy were sitting could probably be easily fixed up with fastened seats for deep-sea fishing.

Yancy said, "The main building's around the other side of the island."

"What's on this side?"

"Storage sheds, power plant, few guest cottages."

"Guest cottages? Customers stay over?" He hadn't been told that.

Yancy shrugged. "Sometimes. Just one night, you know what I mean?"

Parker said, "It's a whorehouse, too, is that it?"

"Not very much." Yancy grinned and spread his hands. "Just sometimes, on a special request, for some good friend of Baron's."

Parker said, "You know Baron?"

Smiling, Yancy shook his head. "I know *about* Baron. That's what counts." He was better than his partner at the wheel in making his speech suit his playboy clothing; only the hard lines of his face gave the lie away.

Parker had been with Yancy off and on the last two days and at all times Yancy carried a glass in one hand and a bottle in the other. Now, discovering the current bottle was empty, he got to

8

his feet and said, "Blast." He flipped the bottle over the side. "Be right back."

Parker watched him go. Yancy moved as though the boat were on dry land and he himself was sober. He went down the ladder into the cabin below and out of sight. Parker watched the island coming closer; he could make out buildings in among the greenery now, small pink cottages near the water and some sort of brick construction farther back.

As Yancy was coming back up on deck with a fresh bottle, the guy at the wheel said, "Somebody coming."

Parker got to his feet. A small boat was chopping through the water toward them, leaving a white Y in its wake.

Yancy said, "No problem, no problem." As though he wanted to soothe his partner at the wheel.

Parker knew the other two looked all right out here, but he in his suit wouldn't ring true. He said, "I'll wait down below."

"Fine, fine." Yancy, distracted, waved the hand with the glass in it. He was watching the little boat speeding toward them.

Parker went below. He was in a fair-sized but crowded room, furnished with a sectional sofa, a chair and table, and a combination kitchenette-bar. Curtained windows lined both sides, giving the interior a dim and bluish light.

Parker went into the aft cabin, more crowded and with a lower ceiling. In one of the closets he found a white yachting cap and a blue jacket like those worn by the two men up on deck. He stripped off his suitcoat and tie, opened his shirt collar, and put on the cap and jacket. Then he went back up on deck.

The smaller boat was just pulling alongside. Three men were in it, all young and hard-looking, wearing dungarees and T-shirts. One of them called, "You people lost?"

Yancy, smiling, holding his bottle and glass, called back, "Not us. Just out for a spin around the park."

The trio in the other boat couldn't be close enough to see the truth on Yancy's face, so they'd have to think they were just looking at an amiable clown. The one that talked said, "You

9

don't want to get too close to the island. Dangerous rocks, things like that. You could ruin your boat."

"Thanks so much." Yancy gestured with bottle and glass. "We'll just sweep around it and hurry on home. Thanks for your concern."

"Remember. Don't get too close."

"I'll remember."

The little boat veered off, heading back for the island. Yancy turned and said, "Very nice. The jacket's a little small, but the cap looks quite sporty."

Parker said, "How many of those has Baron got?"

"What? Boats?"

"Torpedoes."

"Oh." Yancy brushed them aside with an airy wave of the bottle. "Half a dozen, maybe ten. Beach bums."

Parker took the cap and jacket off, dropped them on the chair next to the guy at the wheel. "So far," he said, "it don't look good."

"Love will find a way," Yancy said.

Parker looked at him. Sometimes it seemed as though the face was a lie and the rest was the truth. Yancy was somebody you could underestimate.

The guy at the wheel said, "They still hangin' around, in by shore."

Parker told him, "Go around the island to the left." To Yancy he said, "The brick building there, up behind the cottages. What's that?"

Yancy squinted, behind his sunglasses. "Power plant," he said. "Storage sheds the other side of it, on the far slope. You'll be able to see it better as we go around."

The part of the island Parker had seen so far had no beach, no cove, no pier, no place at all for a boat to come in to shore. Tangled trees and undergrowth clogged the ground right down to the shoreline, and vines and branches overhung the water. The half dozen or so cottages scattered along the slope were all half hidden by the foliage. From not very far away the island

10

would look both uninhabited and uninviting.

The guy at the wheel said, "They're still watching us."

"As we do," Yancy told him, "what I announced we would do. Don't worry about it."

They had started now to make their swing around the island. In close against the island lay the little boat, in the island's shadow, nearly invisible except for the white T-shirts of the three guys who were sitting in there watching.

The island kept looking empty and grim as they went around, until they reached the section exactly opposite the part they'd seen while coming out. Here was the main building, a huge sprawling two-story red brick affair fronted by thick white pillars. Two long piers jutted out into the water, and between them bobbed half a dozen boats like the one Parker was aboard. Careful rock gardens flanked the slate paths up from the piers to the main building, which looked most like an old southern plantation, except that it was practically bare of window.

Yancy said, "The cockfight pit's behind the main building; you can't see it from here. Baron lives in the main building, most of the people that work for him live in that building on the left."

The building on the left was also brick, also two stories high, but plain and functional in design and containing a normal amount of window.

Parker said, "So far, this is the only place we could land."

Yancy nodded. "That's right. Baron cleaned out a channel here."

"So we couldn't land anyplace else."

"That's right."

Parker shook his head. "Bad."

This time, Yancy said nothing.

The guy at the wheel said, "They're following us."

Parker looked behind them, and the little boat was in their wake, but keeping back.

Yancy said, "Ignore them. Go on around."

They went on around the island, and there was nothing else to see. To east and west and south the Gulf of Mexico stretched to the horizon and beyond. To the north the coast was a gray smudge.

Parker said, "Head back."

Yancy gestured with the bottle. "Well? What do you think?"

Parker shook his head.

"It's worth the trouble," Yancy told him.

"Maybe."

A helicopter passed over, coming from the east and heading west. The guy at the wheel squinted up at it: "Is that them, too?"

Yancy laughed. "What, Baron's boys? That's the Navy, U.S. Navy. You think Baron's got helicopters?"

"How should I know?"

Parker was watching aft. The trio in the little boat had dropped out of sight, losing interest. The island again looked empty and uninviting.

Yancy stretched and said, "We'll be back in less than an hour."

Parker looked out toward shore, but they were still too far away to make out any details. Galveston was up that way, ahead of them, but it couldn't be seen yet. Parker turned away and went back down into the cabin. He put his tie and suitcoat on and sat down to wait.

Yancy came down, smiling, easy, relaxed. He sat on the sofa and said, "Well? What do you think?"

"I haven't made up my mind."

"Mr. Karns would be very happy if you thought yes."

Parker looked at him. "Karns doesn't threaten me. Didn't he tell you that?"

Yancy waved glass and bottle. "Wrong, wrong! No threat, just a comment."

Parker went over to the bar and made himself a drink. "I don't have enough yet," he said. "I need more before I can make up my mind."

"Name it."

12

"I want a map of the island. Buildings, paths, landing places, everything."

"It can be arranged."

"And I want a list of personnel. How many, which of them live on the island, what each man's job is, how many of them are heeled, what kind of weapons they got on the island and how many."

"That'll take a little longer."

"But it can be done," Parker said.

Yancy nodded. "It can be done." He smiled again, and motioned with the glass. "One thing I know. Some nights, the handle in that place is a quarter million bucks."

Parker shrugged. It didn't matter how much was there; what counted was how possible it was to take it and leave with it.

He sat down and waited for Galveston.

2

Parker opened the door and Yancy came in, smiling, well dressed, light on his feet. He carried a tan calfskin attaché case, and he looked like an insurance salesman wearing an ape mask. The ape mask opened its smiling mouth and said, "Greetings, I've got it."

Beyond the door the sun beat down white and hot. Parker was staying at a motel on Broadway in Galveston while looking things over and making up his mind. It wasn't the motel he would have chosen for himself, but the reservation had been made for him by Yancy or someone else in Walter Karn's organization; the organization was paying his expenses.

Parker shut the door against the sunlight, leaving the room cool and dim. In the corner the air conditioner hummed to itself. The room looked a lot like the cabin of the boat he was out on yesterday.

Yancy stood in the middle of the room looking around, jiggling his right arm so the attaché case tapped against the side of his knee. "Drink?" he said. "Cold and wet?"

"Don't have any," Parker told him. He itched when he was around steady drinkers; they were unpredictable and unreliable.

Yancy said, "Bad business." He tossed the attaché case on one of the twin beds, went over to the telephone, and stood with it to his ear for a minute. He smiled at Parker, and his right foot tapped on the rug.

"Ah!" he said, into the phone. "This is room twenty-seven. Send me a boy, would you, dear? A million thanks." He cradled the phone and made a gesture of amiable helplessness, saying to Parker, "One of my minor vices. You understand."

Parker shrugged. Understanding had nothing to do with it;

he didn't give a damn, that was all. Yancy wasn't his problem. He motioned at the attaché case. "Let's see it."

"Oh, let's not hurry. Wait till I fortify." Yancy smiled agreeably, twisting his hood's face into an expression it wasn't equipped for, and said, "This is faster service than you expected anyway. Yesterday afternoon on the boat you told me what you wanted, and this afternoon I bring it."

There was a knock at the door. Yancy raised a hand. "There he is." He went over and opened the door and told the boy there, "Jack Daniels, a fifth. You"ll pick it up for me?"

"Yes, sir."

Yancy gave him money. "And a bucket of ice. Do it in under five minutes and the change is yours."

"Yes, sir."

Yancy's smile was the same for everybody; Parker, the bellboy, the three guys yesterday in the other boat. Now he turned it on Parker again and said, "Well, what do you think of Galveston?"

Parker shook his head. He was no good at small talk, because he had no interest in it.

Yancy kept trying. "You haven't seen the night life around here? No? Well, you haven't missed much. Houston's just fifty miles away, of course. Have you been up there?"

Parker turned his back on him, went over to the bed, and picked up the attaché case.

Yancy said, "Not that Houston's so — what are you doing?"

Parker carried the attaché case over to the writing desk, set it down, opened the snaps.

Yancy came over, looking aggrieved, trying to see the funny side of life, saying, "You're in a hell of a hurry, aren't you?"

Parker said, "You want to go out and come in again? I'll wait. Just don't come in here and stand around."

The hail-fellow expressions drained off Yancy's face one by one, as though they'd been painted on in water color and he was standing in the rain. What was left was hard and humorless. "I was told," he said, and all the pretty music was missing from his voice now, too, "I was told to cooperate with you, give you all the help I could, and treat you with kid gloves. I do what I'm told. That's the smart way, do what you're told. But don't push me. Don't push me so far I forget to be smart."

Parker had opened the attaché case. Now he shut it again. "The deal's off. You tell Karns he sent the wrong boy around."

"Wait a second," Yancy said. "Wait a second."

"I got no time," Parker told him, "To sell you insurance, play buddies with you, smile, small talk, how's the weather? I'm here on business."

"We all are," Yancy said, but he seemed less sure of himself.

"I got to have full attention," Parker told him, "on what's in front of me. I can't be worried about you behind me, do you feel well, have you got your bottle, did somebody hurt your feelings?"

"There's a certain civilized procedure," Yancy said. He was flicking in and out of his two characterizations like a candle flame guttering in a wind. "There's a certain civilized way to do things.

"Not here."

They stood looking at each other. Parker didn't necessarily want out of this deal: he didn't know enough about it yet to tell if it was workable or not. But if he couldn't get Yancy squared away he'd quit it now. There was no reason to add unnecessary complications. As they stood there, a knock sounded at the door. Yancy started, then shook his head and said, "My bottle. The boy's fast." He seemed grateful for the interruption.

Parker waited. Yancy went over and opened the door and the boy came in carrying a brown paper bag and a plastic ice bucket. He set them on the table near the door, and Yancy, looking at his watch, said, "Four and a half minutes. The change is yours."

"Thank you, sir."

Parker said, "Boy."

"Sir?"

"How long you work here?"

"Almost three years, sir."

"Any guest here ever hurt your feelings?"

Yancy turned his head and looked at Parker. He and the boy both looked baffled. The boy said, "Sir?"

Parker said, "Somebody wants something, ice or a bottle or carry some luggage. They tell you what they want, they don't say please, they're in a hurry, they don't pay you any mind. That hurt your feelings?"

The boy shook his head. "No, sir."

"Why not?"

The boy looked baffled again. He glanced at Yancy, then looked back at Parker and spread his hands. "Because I work here, I guess, sir."

"You just say, 'Yes, sir.'"

"Yes, sir."

Parker turned to Yancy. "You got it?"

Yancy made an ironic face. "Yes, sir," he said.

"Give the kid another dollar."

"Yes, sir."

Yancy gave the baffled boy a dollar and closed the door after him. He turned to Parker: "You make a strong moral."

"I'm here to look over a job," Parker told him. "That's all, just a job. Not to make pen pals."

Yancy pointed at the bottle. "That won't bother you," he said. "I don't let it get out of hand."

It was time to unbend a little. Parker knew he had Yancy squared away, and the thing to do now was ride out of it and get back to work with no rumpled feelings. He said, "Glass in the bathroom."

Yancy smiled, the old alumnus smile again. "And for you?"

"Small one."

While Yancy went off to get the glasses, Parker opened the attaché case again and took from it a stack of papers. He closed the case, put it on the floor, sat down, and began to spread the papers out on the writing table. Yancy came back with two glasses, put ice and whiskey in them, came across the room, and set one glass down beside Parker's right hand. "Everything you asked for," he said, motioning at the papers. He sounded proud of himself.

One of the papers was a hand-drawn map, on a large sheet of heavy paper that, when opened out, covered the whole surface of the writing desk. The name "COCKAIGNE" had been written across the top, and below it was the island, shaped somewhat like a rubber life raft, with the long dimension running east and west. Whoever had drawn the map had gone to a lot of medieval trouble, drawing tiny buildings on the island, drawing rows of waves and pretty fish jumping out in the ocean, drawing a complex arrow and letter N to show which way was north, even putting a few tiny trees in along the northern shore of the island to show it was all wild there.

This was the trouble with the Outfit, the organization run by Walter Karns. The Outfit had a lot of manpower, a lot of talent, but like every organization on both sides of the law it was so big it sometimes ran for the sake of running, like a man tromping an automobile accelerator to the floor when the gear shift is in neutral; the engine runs fine but the car isn't going anywhere.

The same with this drawing. He'd asked for a map and they gave him a souvenir.

Yancy said, the pride still in his voice, "Well? What do you think of it?"

"Where's the frame?"

"What? Oh, oh yeah, I see what you mean." Yancy laughed a little doubtfully. "Our man kind of got enthusiastic," he said.

"Did he put everything in the right place?" Parker said. "That's the point."

"He's got everything, every detail. You got nothing to worry about there."

Parker pointed at the main building and the living quarters to the left of it. "How far are they apart? What's the scale on this map?"

"Oh," said Yancy. "Oh, for that you want the other map."

"The other map."

Yancy rooted through the papers and came up with a standard-size sheet of graph paper. On it was another rendering

18

of the island, this one simple, bare, and neat. Buildings were shown by numbered rectangles, with a key in the lower right. A notation below this key stated that one square on the graph equaled one thousand feet. Another notation said that the island was forty-seven point three miles from Galveston, and thirty-six point eight miles from the nearest land just north of Surfside, forty miles south of Galveston.

Yancy said, "Is that more like it?"

"Here." Parker gathered up the other map in one hand, crumpling it some, and handed it to Yancy.

"This was supposed to give you more of a picture of the place," Yancy said, defending it.

"I've seen the place," Parker told him. "Sit down and drink."

Yancy sat down. Parker studied the map.

There were fourteen buildings on the island, ranging in size from the large main building by the two piers along the southern edge of the island to the six tiny cottages on the northern slope. In addition to these, there was the building housing employees, and the small building where cock-fights were staged, plus two storage sheds up the slope behind these buildings and the power plant at the top of the island, and finally two small boathouses to the west of the piers, around behind the employees' living quarters.

The boathouses interested Parker. They meant there was a second point where a boat could be brought to shore, away from the exposed main piers. If the operation turned out to be workable, that might come in handy.

He put the map aside and looked at the rest of the papers. On three sheets were listed the names and duties of every employee on the island, plus whether or not they were normally armed and whether or not they lived on the island.

Baron had a large staff working his island; thirty-eight men and eight women. The casino had a staff of fifteen men, four of whom were armed. A chef, four waiters, a bus-boy, and a dishwasher, seven in all, staffed the dining room in the main building. Six men, four of them armed, operated the cockpit. Eight men, four of them armed, operated Baron's fleet of small

19

boats, bringing the customers out from the mainland. Two armed men served as Baron's assistants, adjutants, and bodyguards. Six women were available for specialized cottage service, and two other women worked as maids. In all, including Baron himself, there were forty-seven names on the list.

Of the forty-seven, only seventeen lived permanently on the island itself. Aside from Baron and his two bodyguards, these included the four armed men who worked in the casino, the four armed boatmen, and the six cottage women. Even with everyone else gone, then, there would be eleven armed men on the island at all times.

Other papers gave further information about Baron's empire. It was estimated that between seventy and eighty per cent of Baron's customers came to the island in their own boats, some from as far away as New Orleans and Corpus Christi. For the rest, Baron maintained four fairly large cabin cruisers, each with a crew of two, to shuttle customers from and to Galveston. Two of these boats, manned by the unarmed shore-living boatmen, were based in Galveston, and the two manned by the armed island-living boatmen were based on Cockaigne.

The weapons available on the island were listed on another sheet, and it was an impressive list; rifles and handguns enough to start a revolution, plus tear gas shells and a couple of machine guns.

One page described the approaches to the island. Submerged rocks and reefs, plus steel and concrete additions by Baron, made it impossible to bring a boat of any draft at all in close to shore anywhere except at two points; the main piers in front of the casino, and the boathouses just to the west of the piers.

There were further sheets of facts which Parker either already knew or didn't care about; statistics on numbers of customers, estimated total of money on the island at different times of day and different days of the week and different seasons of the year, police records of Baron's employees. Parker leafed through these, saw there was nothing else of value, and turned to Yancy. "All right," he said. "So far, it doesn't look impossible."

Yancy had been sitting in moody silence on the edge of one of the beds. Now he perked up, stood up, said: "That's good, that's good. Mister Karns will like that."

"So far," Parker repeated.

Yancy was his normal self again, glass in right hand, bottle in left hand, smile on face. He said, "You want something else? Whatever I can do."

"I want to go out there, as a customer."

Yancy seemed surprised. "Really? You want to show your face?"

"Why not?"

"Beats me. It's your face."

It wasn't. It was a face a plastic surgeon had given him once.* But that wasn't the point. "I want to go there," he said. "I'll need a stake, say six hundred."

"Done."

"And a woman. Someone who looks right and knows how to use a camera. With a camera hidden on her someplace, purse or whatever. When I tell her take a picture, she takes a picture."

Yancy nodded. "There's no reason we can't come up with somebody," he said.

"Tonight."

Yancy smiled. "Yes, sir," he said, leaning on the words.

Parker picked out the four or five sheets of paper he'd found useful, and said, "You can take the rest of this stuff away again."

"We like to be thorough," Yancy said.

"So do I," said Parker.

*The Man with the Getaway Face.   21

3

Parker walked around the cab and opened the other door, and the little blonde danced out in a swirl of petticoats and narrow knees and tanned thighs above the stocking tops. She stood patting her waist and studying her purse as Parker shut the door again and the cab drove away.

"To tell you the truth," the blonde said, as Parker took her elbow and they started down the pier, "to tell you the truth, I'm scared to death of water. Terrified. Petrified."

She talked a lot. She'd talked a lot in the cab, and before that she'd talked a lot in his motel room while he was getting ready. She was narrow, narrow all over, with narrow head and narrow waist and narrow legs, and where she wasn't exactly narrow she was at least slender. Her nose was narrow, flanked by prominent cheekbones, and her eyes were large and brown and innocent and liquid, like the eyes of a Walt Disney fawn. She said her name was Crystal, which had to be a lie, and it was impossible she was as brainless as she seemed.

But she looked right for the part, so this time Outfit thoroughness seemed to be working out. If she knew how to operate the camera hidden in her purse, and if she wouldn't do anything stupid to give the game away, fine. In any case, she talked too much.

"I suppose," she said, as they walked down the pier, "it's one of those childhood things? A trauma? Where maybe somebody threw me in the water to teach me to swim and I was too young or something? I don't remember anything like that, but maybe that's significant because I *wouldn't* remember it. That makes sense, doesn't it?"

Parker had discovered the way to handle her. When she paused, he grunted. She turned his grunts into whatever words she wanted to hear, and went on with her monologue again.

"All I know, anyway," she said after his grunt, "all I know for sure is I'm absolutely terrified if I even *think* about water. So I wouldn't come along on a date like this with just anybody, Jerry, let me tell you. This means you're something special, Jerry, that I'd even consent to come out with you like this tonight."

The last two sentences, with the name Jerry in them, had been spoken for the benefit of the stocky guy in the sport shirt and yachting cap at the end of the pier, sitting on a barrel and smoking a cigarette and watching Parker and the girl with complete lack of interest.

Parker stopped and said to the guy, "The boat for Cockaigne leave from here?"

"Where's that?" said the guy.

Parker took from his pocket the small card he'd been given this evening by Yancy. It had written on it in ink, "COCKAIGNE" and "OK" and an illegible signature. Parker handed this to the guy in the yachting cap, who squinted at in in the dim light — two twenty-five watt bulbs glowed high up on a pole at the end of the pier — and then said, "Okay. We leave in five minutes. Go on down the stairs there."

Parker led the way. The stairs were narrow and steep, and the girl didn't have any attention left over for talk until they were down on the deck of the cruiser. Then she said, not loud, "I'm not kidding, I'm really scared. I just hope I don't upchuck, that's all I hope."

Most of the deck was roofed over, and in that area were four rows of chairs, four chairs to each row. Two couples were sitting in the rear row, chatting together quietly. Parker led the way up to the front row and he and the girl sat down there.

Just ahead, three steps led up to a higher level, where the controls were. A guy was sitting on the rail there, a younger version of the stocky type upstairs. He too had a cigarette going, and didn't seem to give a damn about much of anything.

The girl said, "Can you feel the boat move? Feel it? We aren't even going anywhere yet, and it's moving. Can you swim?"

"Yes."

"I can't. Because of my fear, you know? Are you a good swimmer, a real good swimmer?"

"Good enough."

"If this boat sinks or anything, you won't leave me, will you? You'll help me get to shore."

If the boat sank, Parker knew this girl would be hysterical and would drown with her anyone she could get her hands on. If the boat sank, Parker would get as far from her as he could as fast as possible. But he said, "I'll help you. Don't worry about it."

"I can't stop myself, I do worry, that's all. I just can't stop myself." She leaned closer and lowered her voice. "This is stupid, I know it's stupid, but would you mind if I held your hand? Just while we're on the boat, you know? Just for like moral support."

There was nothing else to do. Parker gave her his left hand, and she put into it a hand cold and damp and trembling. She wasn't inventing the fear, it was real. The talk, he supposed, was a way to siphon off some of the nervousness. Maybe most of the time she wasn't a non-stop talker after all.

That was the way the Outfit worked, though. Have a job that means going for a boat ride, get somebody afraid of water. Brilliant.

Four more people came down into the boat, and settled in the row behind Parker and the girl. A minute later the stocky guy came down, cast off the lines, and his younger brother up front started the engine. The girl squeezed Parker's hand, and now she stopped talking. She didn't say a word all the way out to the island.

At night Cockaigne was a lot more impressive. It was just a dark bulk in the water from the landward side, but circling around it the boat abruptly came upon lights and color and the sounds of music.

Spotlights played on the main building and the piers and the surrounding jungle and the water. Colored lights lined both piers just below the water line, making the ocean here look green and red and yellow. Loudspeakers played lush string ensemble music witha fidelity that was surprisingly good for an outdoor system. On the paths and stone benches among the rock gardens between piers and casino sat or strolled a dozen or more of Baron's customers, dark-suited men and bright-gowned women carrying iced drinks and talking together. A score of small boats were docked at the two piers, and at least as many larger boats were anchored offshore, many of them adding their own bright lights and music and laughter.

"My God," said the girl. She seemed to forget for a second her fear of water, but her hand didn't loosen its grip.

There was a reserved space for this shuttle boat at the shoreward end of the lefthand pier, and once they were settled in it the girl hurried ahead of Parker, scrambling up the steps as though the boat were sinking right now. She waited for him on top of the pier, smiling sheepishly.

"I'm sorry," she said, taking his hand in a more relaxed way now. "I tried to keep it in."

"It's all right," he said, although it wasn't. But he'd have to make the effort to keep her in a good mood so she'd do good work.

The ground sloped upward from the pier to the blank-faced brick casino, looking strong and blind up there with its white pillars and its lack of window. The rock gardens through which they had to walk to get to the casino had an intricate, fussy, Japanese look about them, full of varicolored odd-shaped stones and tiny gnarled bushes. The stone benches here and there were gray, weathered, like Aztec ruins. Farther along, knotted jungle growth filled the slope up behind the casino, framing it in dark green.

As they moved away from the pier, Parker said, his voice low, "Start taking pictures."

"I already took two," she said. "One coming in and one on the pier."

He was surprised. "Good," he said.

"Don't worry, I'll do my job."

He believed her.

Tall broad glass doors led into the casino. Outside the night had a tropical heat and mugginess to it, but inside there was the coolness and dryness of air conditioning.

The glass doors had led them into a large high-ceilinged anteroom. The walls were a pale cream color, the far ceiling iced with hanging glass chandeliers, the floor a checkerboard of huge black and white tile squares. Renaissance paintings hung on the walls, and dark wood antique chairs and love seats were spotted here and there along the sides of the room.

Broad arched open doorways led off on three sides, each with an identification in black discreet block letters on the wall above the arch. To the left, the dining room. Straight ahead, what were gently termed lounges. To the right, the casino proper.

Parker said, "Food now or later?"

"Later. When my nerves calm down."

"This way, then."

Parker and the girl went through the archway on the right, into the casino.

The ceiling here was lower, and modernistic; acoustical tile spaced with inset fluorescent light fixtures. The walls were pool-table green, done in a fabric wallpaper. The floor was carpeted in a darker green. Gaming tables were set at random throughout the room, facing this way and that in a careful, tasteful simulation of disorder. To the left, behind gleaming mahogany and a brass wire mesh, stood the cashiers, in black sleevebands and green eyeshades.

Parker bought two hundred dollars' worth of chips, gave the girl a hundred, and spent some time moving around the room. He won a little at a crap table, betting against the point, lost a little on the red at roulette, won and lost and won again at *chemin de fer*.

There were no slot machines, only gaming tables of every kind. Parker and the girl stood at a poker table till a chair became free, and then the girl sat down and played half a dozen hands. She won a large pot with jacks full, squealed with joy, kissed the cards, clutched handfuls of chips to her breast. She called attention to herself, but in a good way, in a way that called no attention to the man with her. She played the sexy, naive, gold-digging, wide-eyed blonde to the hilt, and the looks she got were compounds of amusement and lust.

After an hour they moved on to the dining room, where the food was viciously expensive but superb. The dining room was huge, but broken up by vine-grown trellises and flower-filled planters. A fountain in the middle of the room plashed quietly, and the waiters moved with silent speed.

Nowhere did he see a way to the second floor, no unexplained doors anywhere. There had to be more to the building, downstairs as well as up, but he couldn't yet figure out the internal arrangement. Exits from the dining room led only to the entrance hall, to the lounges, and to the kitchen. From the casino there was an exit only to the entrance hall, and the men's lounge was also a cul-de-sac, opening only onto the entrance hall. The girl told him the same was true of the women's lounge.

Back in the casino, Parker left the girl at a crap table while he roamed around the room. The only answer was a hidden door, and this was the room most likely to contain it. Why Baron would have installed a secret door to the second floor when obviously the place had to have a way to get upstairs Parker couldn't guess, but it was clear that Baron had done so.

It took him fifteen minutes to find. A thin vertical line in the baseboard at one point along the rear wall was the give-away. The door sat so flush with the wall that no line or break in the wallpaper could be seen from more than a foot away, but down at the baseboard the joining wasn't quite so perfect.

Parker didn't stop to inspect the door; it would have to be under observation. In the next fifteen minutes he strolled slowly by it six times, studying it, finding no way to open it from this side. It would have to be controlled electrically from somewhere else, probably the cashier's wicket.

Five minutes later he'd taken the girl away from the crap table and she'd had three shots of the section of wall with the door in it. Then they left the building and took the slate path around the right to the cockpit at the rear. The path was lined by thick hedges, separating them from a narrow path of lawn and then the dense jungle.

On the way around, she said, "I've never seen a cockfight. Do you mind if I take a couple pictures of it, just for myself?"

"Go ahead."

The cockpit was in a small, round, brick, windowless building with a green conical roof directly behind the casino. It looked like a truncated silo. Old-fashioned carriage lamps hung all around the building, and more lamps of the same style on black metal poles flanked the path.

There was an admission charge to the cockpit: five dollars a head. Inside, steeply slanted tiers of seats formed a circle around the smallish dirt area in the middle. It looked like an operating amphitheater, or a miniature bull ring.

A fight was already in progress, the birds' handlers calling to them in Spanish, the commissioners walking around and around the tiers calling out the odds and taking bets. There were two closed metal exit doors in addition to the door Parker had just come in.

The tiers were less than half full, and most of the customers looked like people seeing their first cockfight and neither understanding nor liking anything of what they saw. Here and there aficionados shouted encouragement and jargon in English or Spanish.

There was no money here. This was a gimmick, a touch of exotica to bring the customers in. It looked cheap and fly-by-night, a marginal operation. The money was all in the other building, in the casino.

Parker spent a few minutes looking the place over and then left. The girl came along, but reluctantly, staring back into the pit all the time they were climbing to the doorway. Outside, she held Parker's arm and leaned against him. Breathily she said, "I never knew . . . I didn't know there was anything like that." Her eyes gleamed in the lamplight, her feet seemed unsteady on the path as they walked back around toward the casino entrance again.

She said, "Wasn't it incredible? Wasn't it fascinating?"

"Mm."

"I never saw anything. . . I could stay there all night, look at me, I'm trembling all over. Where were they from, are they from Mexico?"

"Yes."

"The men, too? The ones talking to them?"

"Handlers. Trainers. Baron imports them with their birds."

"I've never been to Mexico," she said, thoughtfully. And then, as they were entering the main building again, "Do they have them in Mexico a lot? Cockfights?"

"Here and there."

They went inside and he left her at one of the tables again, with instructions to get some pictures of the cashier's wicket. He went away to the roulette table nearest the cashier and played off and on while watching the routine behind the wire, where the cash went, who did what, what keys opened the wood and wire door in the far corner.

After half an hour he gathered up the girl again and they went back outside. This time they followed the path around the other way, down between the main building and the living quarters, past the cockpit on the other side, and up between the storage sheds. The path was just dirt here, hemmed in by jungle, scantily lit by bare bulbs hanging by wires from tree branches.

Just past the storage sheds a heavy-set man in a dark suit stepped out on the path in front of them. "Sorry, friends," he said. "No guests past this point."

Parker took from his pocket a ten dollar bill. "A little walk and privacy," he said, "that's all we're looking for." He stepped forward with his hand out, and the bill disappeared.

The heavy-set man said, "Don't go in none of the cottages, though. I can't do nothing about that. You go in there, you get us all in trouble."

"We'll keep out."

29

The heavy-set man moved back into the darkness and Parker and the girl moved on.

The path now detoured around the power plant, a bulky humming building in semidarkness. Around on the other side the ground sloped downward, and now the path, just barely lit by widely spaced dim bulbs, meandered and curved back and forth, passing one after another of the cottages. The cottages were flimsy pastel clapboard structures of the tourist-cabin type, built up on concrete block supports to keep the damp away, and with narrow porches equipped with hammocks. Just enough land had been cleared for each cottage, so the jungle hemmed it in on all sides and the path skirted the porch steps. All the cottages were dark and seemed empty.

At the sixth cottage the path ended. "Wait here," said Parker. He took a pencil flash from his pocket and tried groping through the underbrush toward the water, but it was impossible. He could catch occasional glimpses of the ocean out there, glinting in the moonlight, but the undergrowth was too dank and thick and interwoven for any sort of passage short of chopping one's way with a machete.

Parker said, "All right." He put the pencil flash away again. "Let's go back."

"You want any pictures?"

"Of what? There's nothing here."

They retraced their steps, this time seeing nothing of the heavy-set man, and when they got back to the main building Parker turned and led the way past the living quarters, down a concrete walk behind the living quarters to the two boathouses.

Two of the three young men who'd come out in the small boat yesterday were sitting on webbed lawn chairs by one of the boathouses, dressed the same way as before. One of them got up and came over to Parker and the girl, saying, "Off limits. You want to go the other way."

"Sorry," said Parker. He stood there looking at the boathouses and the water. "Nice place here," he said.

The guy didn't know exactly what to do. He didn't want to

get tough or rude with a customer, but he knew he was supposed to keep people away from here. He took another step forward, holding his arms out as though to keep Parker from seeing anything or getting by him, and said, "I'm sorry, but orders is orders. You got to go back to the casino."

"Sure," said Parker. He turned away, taking the girl's arm, and when they'd walked out of earshot he said, "You get pictures?"

"Four of them."

"We're done. You ready for another boat ride?"

"Not really, but let's get it over with."

They had to wait in the boat ten minutes, with the girl getting more and more shaky the whole time, talking faster and louder, jabbering away like a disc jockey, and once again she shut up the second the boat pulled away from the dock and was silent the whole trip.

There were three empty cabs parked along the curb near the pier entrance. As they came out, the girl, somewhat recovered again, said, "Come on along to my place, I'll develop these pictures right now. You can have them in an hour."

"Good." Parker opened the door of the lead cab, and they got aboard. She gave a LaMarque address and they sat in silence as the cab headed for Galveston Bay and the Gulf Freeway.

Her apartment was in a large modern elevator building with central air conditioning. He windows overlooked no view at all, but were large anyway. The living room was expensively and tastefully decorated, but with the sterility and lack of individuality of a display model.

"Bar over there," she said, pointing. "Just let me get this film started. You could make me a martini, if you would."

"Sure."

"Very very dry."

She went through the archway on the far side of the room, and Parker went over to the bar, a compact and expensive-looking piece of furniture in walnut. It included a miniature refrigerator containing mixers and an ice cube compartment and up above a wide assortment of bottles and glasses.

Parker made the martini with the maximum of gin and the minimum of vermouth, and added an olive from a jar of them in the refrigerator. For himself he splashed some I.W. Harper over ice.

Then he had nearly ten minutes to wait, and waiting was something he'd never learned how to do. He prowled the living room like a lion in a cage, this way and that, back and forth. He carried his drink and took occasional small bites from it.

There were paintings on the walls, small ones, originals, abstracts with the primary color paints piled on thick and messy, the frames neat and plain and simple. They looked like things bought at an annual sidewalk art show; none of them distracted Parker from his pacing more than a few seconds.

The furniture was bland, dull, pastel, straight out of a foam rubber store's show window, but quietly and discreetly and tastefully expensive. The carpeting, the wallpaper, the light fixtures and draperies, all showed the same grasp of fashion and the same total lack of individuality.

This was much worse than waiting in a motel room or someplace like that. This place was dry but awkward, like a desert with green sand.

Crystal, whatever her name was, came back in a bright print blouse and black stretch pants and flat shoes. "I just had to change," she said. "I felt so stiff in that dress. My drink?"

He was near the bar. He picked up her drink and handed it to her, and she said, "Thanks. Let me know when it's fifteen minutes, I'll have to go move the film from A to B." She tasted the drink and raised her eyebrows to show delight. "Mmmm! You have a talent."

"How long before we get pictures?"

"About an hour. Why, are you in a hurry to be off?" She smiled over her drink, showing white teeth, and batted her eyes a little.

Parker shrugged. "No hurry," he said. He turned away and went back over to the bar to refresh his drink.

She followed him, saying, "I guess you're what they call the strong silent type. No idle chitchat, no passes, just business."

"That's right."

"But business is over tonight," she said. She was standing very close behind him.

He turned around. "When did they move you in here?"

She was startled. "What?"

"I figure three months ago," he said. "Long enough so you've set up your darkroom, but not long enough to change anything in here."

"What are you talking about?"

He said, "I figure Karns didn't send you after me, that's some local boy's idea. Karns is too smart for that."

She looked at him, frowning a bit now, studying him. She sipped at her martini and said, "Why? I'm the wrong type?"

"You're the wrong information," he told her. "I'll decide yes or no, and it's what the island looks like that says which it is. Karns could give me three women a night for a month and it would still be what the island looks like that would make me say yes or no about the job, and Karns is smart enough to know that."

She decided to be coldly insulted. "You think Mr. Karns *gave* me to you?"

"No. I think some local bright boy did it and Karns'll talk to him when he hears about it."

"What if I tell you you're wrong? What if I tell you I was just sent along to take your pictures for you, and I got intrigued by you and curious about you, and I thought I might like to find out about you? What if I told you it was all my idea?"

Parker said, "How much did that chair cost you?"

"What chair?" She was annoyed at the change of subject.

Parker pointed. "That one. How much?"

"How do I know?" She looked at the chair and shook her head. "What difference does it make?"

"The difference," he said, "is this isn't an apartment, this is a crib."

"A what?"

"Crib. It's a place where whores work."

"You—" She was insulted again, and this time it seemed more real. She stepped back a pace, saying, "I ought to throw this drink in your face."

"This isn't your apartment," he said. "This is where you entertain for the Outfit."

"What a damn lie!"

Parker shrugged. "You can send me the pictures," he said. He drained his glass, put it down, and headed for the door.

He was almost to it before she spoke, and then she sounded almost plaintive, all the anger and irritation gone: "Why did you do this? Why act this way? You didn't have to."

He wanted the pictures. He turned and said, "I think I did." To get the pictures sooner, he'd talk to her, explain to her.

She said, "If it wouldn't make any difference which way you decided about the other thing, then why not go ahead? You're putting something over, you're getting something for nothing."

"A prize," he said. "A prize for being stupid. And I don't even have to be really stupid, I just have to play like I'm stupid."

"In other words," she said, "it's pride. You thought you were being under-rated and it hurt your pride."

He shook his head. "Whores," he said, "are for people without resources. I don't need you on your terms."

"Oh?" She frowned, studying him, and then she nodded and said, "Oh. All right. If that's the way — I suppose you've guessed I was supposed to phone in my report right after you left."

He nodded.

"One minute," she said. She crossed the room to the telephone, dialed a number, waited, and said, "Crystal here. He just left. No dice." She waited again, looking at Parker, and said into the phone. "He tumbled, that's why. The apartment looked phony, and I guess I did it wrong myself."

Parker went over and took the phone away from her and

34

listened, hearing a male voice say, ". . . won't need it. But I'm surprised at. . ." He handed it back, and she took over the conversation again, saying she was sorry a couple of times and then ending it.

She cradled the phone and looked at Parker. "Do you want me to send the pictures or will you wait for them?"

"I'll wait for them."

"What were you drinking?"

"Harper."

While she made him a fresh drink she said, "You know, I'm not conning you now. Do you know that?"

He sat down on the sofa. "Yes."

"How can you be sure?"

"Because," he told her, "you can be sure you can't do anything about my yes or no, no matter what happens here. If I stay, if I go, no matter what, you won't have any reason to make another call."

She nodded. "That's right." She came over and handed him his glass and sat down beside him. "That's right," she said. She smiled; she had an elfin smile, a pixie smile. "And if now I told you it's just that I'm intrigued about you and curious about you, and I'd like to find out about you, what would you say?"

The terms were better now. He put his drink down and reached for her.

4

He rolled over under the sheet and put his hand on her thigh and rubbed upward, putting some pressure in it, rubbing upward over her belly and breasts to her shoulder, then putting his hand back down to her thigh and rubbing upward once again. Her flesh was warm and dry and resilient.

The second time he did it she made a moaning sound deep in her throat, and squirmed under his hand, and moved her arms in a lazy way. The third time, she opened her eyes as though surprised.

"Oh!" she said. She blinked rapidly, and yawned, and stretched her arms up so her breasts were pulled taut. He stroked his hand across them and she laughed and said, "It's you! Good morning!"

"Not yet," he said.

"Oh? Oh! Oh, yes, of course. . ." She held her arms out to receive him. "Yes, of course," she murmured.

The pattern was changing here, but he understood why. His sexual appetite was cyclical, at its peak right after a job, waning slowly, disappearing entirely when he was involved in the planning and preparation of the next job. According to that pattern he should be having little or no interest in Crystal right now. But the usual pattern was based on his working only once or twice a year, and that was where the difference lay; the football stadium heist★ had only taken place six weeks ago. He was working again so soon because of a combination of an unusual need for money and the timely request from Walter Karns. So, for one of the few times in his life, he was combining business with pleasure.

★*The Seventh*, Pocket Book edition 50244.

As they were getting out of bed, she said, "Did you get an answer on your call yet?"

He'd put in a call last night, after he'd looked over the pictures, to Grofield's contact. "No," he said. "It's still too early." Grofield mostly liked to sleep till noon.

She said, "Does it mean you're going to do it? Making the call, does that mean—?"

"Stop working," he said.

She no longer took offense with him. She just laughed and shook her head. "I'm not working, I'm curious. I want to know for myself."

"You're curious all the time."

"All right, never mind. May I ask what you want for breakfast?"

"I don't care," he said. "Whatever you make." Food was functional with him, he didn't think about it.

She said, "There's one thing I've got to say."

"Say it."

"I'd like you to stay here, as long as you want. But if you stay, I'll have to tell my boss, so he won't give me anything else to do."

Parker considered. It would take a week or two to get set up, and the choice was between here and the motel room. After he was more fully involved in the job the usual pattern might reassert itself, but until then this place had advantages over the motel. He said, "Tell your boss to have somebody pick up my stuff at the motel and bring it here."

"Good."

She made breakfast while he showered, and afterward they went back to bed for a while. Someone brought Parker's suitcase a little after ten and Crystal's nesting instinct took over. She had to unpack everything and stow everything away, and then she had to get dressed and take things down to the cleaners. While she was gone Parker looked over some of the pictures again — they were all first-rate black and white prints — and when she came back he took her clothing off and returned her to bed.

The phone rang at eleven-thirty. They were sitting up, smoking cigarettes, and she reached to the bedside extension, spoke into it, and then passed the phone to Parker, saying, "It's for you. Thank him for not calling five minutes ago."

Parker said, "Hello."

"Was that a lady I heard, with that bedroom voice?"

"Grofield?"

"Talking to you is like having a chat with one of the statues on Easter Island. How are you, Parker?"

It was Grofield, always amusing himself with his own dialogue. But he was a good man, reliable on a job and perfect for this one. Parker said, "There's an investment you might be interested in."

"Having just had a theater shot out from under me by the Philistines, I can tell you your statement is succinct and pithy but perhaps underplayed."

"You'll like this one. Unlimited front money and guaranteed return."

"Two impossibilities in one sentence. I'm intrigued."

"How soon can you get here?"

"This afternoon. I'm in New Orleans."

Parker gave him the address of Crystal's apartment, and Grofield said, "Full explanations when I get there, Parker, none of your bloody monosyllables."

"All right."

Parker gave the phone back to Crystal, thinking the explanation on this job would take a long time in the telling. But that was later. He stubbed out his cigarette and said, "Better leave the phone off the hook."

5

It was hard to tell where the explanation should start. This job had come along because of Parker's connection with the Outfit, which was what the organized rackets boys were calling themselves these days, so maybe the beginning of the explanation was how Parker first got involved with the Outfit.

Parker and the Outfit had one thing in common; they both worked outside the law. But the Outfit lived on gambling and narcotics and prostitution, the Outfit lived by finding customers for illegal products and services, and Parker simply went where money was and took it away. He scored once or twice a year, almost always institutional robberies — banks, payrolls, jewelry stores, armored cars — and almost always with a group of three or four other professionals in the same line of work. The personnel of the group would change from job to job, depending on who was lining up the string and what the operation required. Over the last nineteen years Parker had worked with about a hundred different men.

One of these men, Mal Resnick, had worked a doublecross in a job with Parker, and had used Parker's share to pay back an old debt to the Outfit. Parker had caught up with Resnick and settled accounts, but he'd had to exert pressure to get his money back from the Outfit.* A man named Bronson had been running the Outfit then, and when Bronson had insisted on trying to have Parker killed, Parker had worked an arrangement with the man in line to succeed Bronson, a guy named Walter Karns. Parker had eliminated Bronson, and Karns had called off the feud.*

Now he had heard from Karns again, a roundabout message asking only that Parker meet with Karns in Las Vegas. The message had included plane fare and had hinted at a large

*Point Blank.
*The Outfit.

amount of money, so Parker went.

They met in a hotel suite on the Strip; it was their first meeting face to face. They were both big men, Parker thirty-eight and Karns ten or fifteen years older. The difference between them was that Parker looked to be made of chunks of wood, while Karns had a meaty padded look to him, like a wrestler gone to seed.

'The situation is simple," Karns said. "We've got a competitor and we don't like competitors. Mostly we take care of competitors ourselves, but this is an unusual case. It's so unusual I've decided maybe we ought to ask you to take care of the problem for us."

"I don't kill for hire," Parker told him.

"Don't I know that? Don't I have boys who do, a payroll choked with them? No, Parker, I don't want you for a job I could get done better by any one of a dozen people on my own payroll. I want you for the kind of job you do best, I want you for your specialty. I want you to rob this competition, I want you to clean him out, strip him to the bone, leave him naked."

"Why?"

Karn shrugged. "Because there's no other way we can get at him."

"Why not?"

"Now you're asking the question, now you've touched on the main point. What is it that makes this problem unique? Did you ever hear of the island of Cockaigne?"

"No."

"It's in the Gulf of Mexico, off the Texas coast, about forty or fifty miles south of Galveston. Up till six years ago it was deserted, nobody on it, nothing there anybody wanted. Nobody owned it. It's forty miles from the United States and about two hundred and thirty from Mexico, but neither one of them ever wanted it bad enough to stake a claim. It was such a nothing the Seabees didn't even build an airfield on it in the Second World War, which makes it almost the only one they missed."

Karns pulled at his gin and tonic. "Then," he said, "along

came a guy named Baron. Wolfgang Baron, that's what he calls himself. He showed up on the island with nothing but time and money. He hired construction crews out of Galveston to come out and build him a casino and some other buildings, and when the Feds took a look at him it turned out Cuba had just finished going through the paperwork at the UN and the island was theirs. So the Galveston construction crews quit on him, and he brought Mexican crews up from Matamoros instead and they finished the job. When everything was done he called the place Cockaigne, because it never even had a name before, and he opened for business."

Karns finished his drink and hollered. A sallow young guy in a black suit came in from another room and made fresh drinks for both Karns and Parker; then he went out again.

Karns said, "You ever hear this name before, Cockaigne?"

Parker shook his head.

"One of my lawyers told me what it is," Karn said. "There was an old legend in the old days in England about a country called Cockaigne where everything was great. Streets made of sugar, doughnuts growing on the trees and like that. Like the song about the big rock candy mountain. Idleness and luxury, that was Cockaigne, and that was what this bird Baron called his gambling island."

Parker didn't care about legends in the old days in England. What he cared about was what Karns wanted from him right now. But he knew the only thing to do with these people full of unimportant details was wait them out; sooner or later they'd get to the point.

Karns was saying now, "You see what this guy Baron had in mind, something like the old gambling ships used to stay just outside the twelve-mile limit, we used to operate a couple of them ourselves, but with Baron it's more complicated than just a ship. He finds himself an island situated just right, makes a deal with a country to claim it and then leave him alone with it, and he's set. He gets a lot of his business from the yacht and small boat trade in the Gulf, and the rest of it from the rich

41

Texans. They come from Houston and San Antonio and Corpus Christi and Austin. They come from as far away as Dallas and New Orleans. They spend money on that God damn island like the stuff was going out of style, and not a penny of it comes to us."

Karns got to his feet, began to pace the room. His face and voice and movements showed him feeling again an old irritation that hadn't eased with time. "For six years," he said, "that son of a bitch has sat out there and laughed at us. We told him he couldn't operate without us, we offered him a fifty-fifty split, and he told us to go to hell. He never moves off that island so we can get at him, and as long as he's on the island he's safe from us. We can't pressure him with our own law people because he's outside everybody's jurisdiction."

Parker said, "So you want me to take his money away."

"Right. I want you to pluck him like a chicken, scrape him clean. Don't just rob the place, burn it to the ground, rip it right off that God damn island and throw it in the sea. Gut it, like Couffignal. Or don't you know that one either?"

Parker didn't. He said, "What's in it for me?"

Karns spread his hands. "Whatever's on the island. He must have a million stashed there by now, maybe more."

Parker shook his head. "The guy you've been describing isn't stupid. He's got a week's proceeds there at the most and you know it. The rest is in Swiss banks."

Karns shrugged. "It's a possibility, I admit it. But even a week's proceeds will be plenty."

"How much?"

Karns squinted into the middle distance, finally said, "I suppose about a quarter million."

"Make that a guarantee," Parker said.

"What?" Karns turned to look at him. "How could I do that? You want me to send accountants in?"

"You make up the difference," Parker told him. "We go there, do the heist, burn the place down like you want, and you make up the difference between our take and a quarter million."

"Well, now," Karns said. "Well, now, wait a minute. That's liable to be a lot of money. I don't think I could go along with that."

"You called for me because you need a professional in my line of work. When you want a professional you've got to pay for him."

"Well, of course, I know that, but still and all. Two hundred fifty thousand dollars is a lot of money."

"It was your figure," Parker reminded him.

"For a top," Karns said. "I was estimating how *much* it might be."

"Estimate an average."

Karns frowned, looking like a man with an ulcer. It was obvious he didn't want to pick a number low enough for Parker to figure the job wasn't worth it, but on the other hand he didn't want to pick a number high enough for his organization to have to make up the difference between it and the actual take. Finally he said, "For an average, for what I'd guess would be the average general amount of cash you might find on the island, I'd say a hundred and eighty thousand."

"Say two twenty," Parker told him.

Karns looked surprised, and then laughed. "Are we haggling? Do we settle at two hundred thousand?"

Parker said, "Plus front money."

"What? What front money?"

"Every job," Parker told him, "has expenses beforehand. There's weapons to buy, other things. If this is an island, we'll need a couple of boats."

"We can supply everything," Karns assured him.

But Parker shook his head. "No. We buy everything before the job, use it once, destroy it afterwards. That way there's no links between us and the job."

"This time," Karns said, "you won't have to worry about things like that. There's no law out at the island, no one will ever be after you for this job."

"It isn't my first job," Parker said, "and it won't be my last. I won't leave things around."

"In other words, you'll do it your way or not at all."

"Yes."

"Is it all right if we supply the material and leave its disposition up to you?"

Parker shrugged. "Just so you don't expect anything back."

"I understand that. All right, so you'll do it for guaranteed two hundred thousand dollars take, plus material."

"If the job can be done," Parker said.

"You mean it isn't an agreement yet?"

Parker shook his head. "Not till I look it over. If I don't think I can do it, there's no deal."

Karns spread his hands. "Then look it over," he said. "By all means look it over."

Now Parker had looked it over, and the job seemed possible, and he had made his first contact to build the string for the operation. He was working again.

TWO

1

Grofield came in saying, "I'll take the job only if the place we knock over is air conditioned. Have you felt that *heat* out there? How are you, Parker?"

They shook hands. Parker said, "I haven't been out today."

"Nor would I be," said Grofield, catching sight of Crystal. "Darling," he told her, "you are everything my heart desires. Fly with me."

"I can't," she said. "High altitudes give me nosebleeds."

"My nosebleeds come from my wife," Grofield said, and grinned ruefully. To Parker he said, "Did you know I married that darling little telephone girl? A natural actress, natural actress. You should see her in *Hedda Gabler.*"

Grofield had picked up the telephone girl in the course of the last job he'd worked with Parker, in a place called Copper Canyon.* Parker said, "Good. Now she can't testify against you."

"A romantic," Grofield said. "Parker, you are a true romantic, Robin Hood in the age of mechanization."

Parker said, "Sit down. Let's talk about the job."

"Is honeypot here in the know?"

"Don't worry about her," Parker said.

"I'll go to the supermarket," Crystal said. She smiled at Grofield. "Nice to have met you."

"Polygamy," Grofield told her, "is the only answer."

Grofield watched Crystal leave the room, and then he settled with a grateful sigh on the sofa, spreading his legs out in front of him. He was a tall man, lean and sleek, with carefully tended wavy black hair, urbane good looks, an air of easy competence about him. He was a sometime actor, sometime roadshow producer, and he financed his theatrical career with the money he made in his other line of work, taking

**The Score.*

47

jobs with men like Parker.

He said, "Tell me the story," and he meant he was finished clowning around. It was his saving grace, as far as Parker was concerned; he knew when to get down to business.

Parker told him the situation in brief, explaining as quickly and basically as he could, and Grofield's questions were few and to the point. When the Karns connection with the job was explained, Parker showed him the map of the island and the photos Crystal had taken.

Grofield said, "Good-looking layout. I think it'll be tough to take."

"Maybe not."

Grofield said, "Show me."

"I don't have a plan cold yet. But I figure we come in two ways. A couple of guys come in like regular customers, down to the main pier. When they get a chance they move over to the boathouses, clean out anybody on guard there, and the others come in that way with the boat we use for the getaway. Karns wants the place burned down, and that's good, we make a lot of confusion, a lot of panic, we get away clean underneath it."

Grofield said, "How many men you figure?"

"Four or five, maybe more."

"So it's probably around forty thousand apiece."

"Around that."

"How much can you count on this guy Karns?"

"You mean, will he welsh on the guarantee?"

Grofield nodded. "Or pull a doublecross and try to heist the heisters."

"No. Karns knows me from before, he won't try anything."

"I'll take your word for it." Grofield glanced at some of the pictures again. "I guess you figure me one of the guys coming in the front way."

"Right."

"And you the other one?"

"Yes."

Grofield shook his head. "You run the boathouse brigade,"

he said. "I can look sensible going to a place like that alone, but you can't. Without a woman on your arm, you'd look like forty kinds of trouble."

He was right and Parker knew it. He said, "Who, then?"

"How about Salsa?"

Salsa had also worked with them on the Copper Canyon job. He had a gigolo's looks and a gigolo's background. Grofield was right; Salsa would be perfect for the front way. Parker said, "You want to contact him?"

"Sure. What else do we need?"

"A peterman and somebody knows boats."

"Peterman. But you don't know what kind of safe."

"It's got to be upstairs," Parker said, "and I couldn't get up there anyway."

"I don't like that secret panel garbage, if you want the truth. I figure something like that's always around for a reason, and I figure I don't know yet what the reason is."

"We'll know when we crack it," Parker told him. He wasn't worried about that door himself; it couldn't lead anywhere but upstairs, and upstairs couldn't have too many surprises.

Grofield said, "What we want is an all-around safeman, somebody can handle the box no matter what it is."

"There aren't many of them," Parker said. "Not any more. Dead or retired, all the old juggers."

"There's a guy I worked with a couple years ago," Grofield said thoughtfully. "To look at him you wouldn't think he had a brain in his head. He's a wrassler, one of those TV boys with all the hair, he looks like an abominable snowman. But you should see him with a safe, he's got the touch of a Florence Nightingale."

"What's his name?"

"Gruber. Gropin' Gruber I always called him."

"I've heard of a safeman called Gruber, but I never met him."

"If you heard he was good, it's the same man."

"Can you get in touch with him?"

"I think so. I'll try tonight, when I put in the call for Salsa. And what else?"

"Someone to run the boat."

Grofield shook his head. "That's a funny one. I've never been on a job where we needed a boat."

"Maybe Salsa knows somebody. Or your friend Gruber."

"What about Joe Sheer? He knows just about everybody."

Parker shook his head. "He's dead," he said. Joe Sheer had handled Parker's messages for years, ever since Joe retired from his main business, opening safes. "He died a few months ago," Parker said.

"Is that right? Old Joe? I liked him, Parker, I honest to God liked that old man. What, was it sudden?"

"It was sudden," Parker said. He was leaving out a lot, that Joe Sheer's death had caused Parker trouble and ultimately destroyed the usefulness of the safe cover identity Parker had used on his off-work time for years.* It was because of that bad time that Parker now needed money badly enough to work two operations in less than two months.

Grofield said, "All right. I'll ask around. We'll want a man who can do more than just run a boat, won't we?"

"I figure, the way we'll work it, we ought to leave him at the boathouses to cover our getaway route. You and Salsa and me, we get Gruber into the casino and upstairs to the safe."

"All right. We want a driver, in other words, except it's a boat driver."

Crystal came in as Grofield was talking. "Boats," she said. "Don't talk about boats. I'm still not recovered."

"You take first-rate pictures," Grofield told her. "How are you on publicity photos? I've been needing new ones."

"Carry this bag to the kitchen," she said. "We'll talk about it."

The other two went into the kitchen and Parker sat on the sofa, bent over the map lying on the coffee table. He could visualize the way it was, the way it would be. There was still work to do, preparation, but they were started.

*The Jugger.

Out in the kitchen, Grofield was flirting with his woman. He didn't hear it.

2

Yancy said, "It's the red one there." He pointed at a red Thunderbird glinting in the sunlight, a new hardtop with a broken tail-light.

Parker walked with him across the sidewalk from Crystal's apartment house to the car. The heat was bright, heavy, oppressive, especially after the air conditioned building. They got into the car and Yancy started the engine and turned a switch on the dashboard. "All the comforts of home," he said, meaning the car was air conditioned.

They drove over Texas Avenue to the Gulf Freeway and headed north. Yancy turned on the radio and found a station playing the top forty. The radio started the second it was switched on, with no wait for warmup, and at the push of a button it moved along the dial and stopped automatically when it found a station.

The car was so full of gimmicks it was a surprise it would move at all. Tinted glass, tachometer, compass, joy knob. Large foam rubber dice hung from the rearview mirror. A stuffed toy tiger sat on the shelf by the back window. Mirrors were mounted on both fenders. Round large extra brake lights flanked the toy tiger.

It was thirty-five miles to the end of the Freeway at Dowling Avenue in Houston. They did it in twenty-eight minutes, silently, each thinking his own thoughts. Off the Freeway, Yancy drove over to Washington Street and stopped in front of a seedy bar called Tropical Palm Lounge. "This is the place," he said, and got out of the car.

Parker followed him inside. The interior was a large square room full of round little tables with shiny black formica tops. Posts here and there were surfaced with amber-tinted mirrors. A small stage at the back contained an upright piano, a set of drums with DW in large letters on the bass drum, and a microphone. A narrow dancing area enclosed by a low wooden rail was in front of the stage, and the bar, backed by more amber-tinted mirrors, was along the left wall.

The time was early afternoon, and the place was nearly deserted. One bartender was on duty, with three customers to keep him company at the bar. The tables were all empty, and no waiter or waitress was in sight.

Yancy said, "This way." He went first to the bar, saying, "Hi, Eddie."

"Whadaya say, Yancy?"

"Bottle in the back, boy?"

"Sure thing, Yancy."

"You're my pal." He turned to Parker and motioned with his head. "Come on."

Yancy was enjoying himself, being the big man on the local scene showing off for the out-of-towner. It didn't bother Parker. Just so Yancy did what he was supposed to do, he could choose any style he liked.

They walked now down the length of the bar and through a door at the back marked "Office." But the door didn't lead to an office, it led to a short hall with doors to left and right. The door on the left also said "Office," but it was through the door on the right that Yancy led the way.

They were in a storeroom, piled high with cases of liquor. At a small table in a cleared space near the door sat a short stocky man with snow-white hair and the red-veined nose of an alcoholic. He had been playing solitaire. An ashtray on the table was mounded high with cigarette butts.

Yancy said, "Hey, there, Humboldt. How's it going?"

Humboldt said, "You got a cigarette, Yancy? I run out." He had a nasal voice, a whiner's voice, full of grievance and complaint. The voice went with a smaller thinner body than Humboldt's.

Yancy said, "They got a whole machine up front. You run the place yourself, cop a pack."

"I didn't feel like walkin' all the way out."

Yancy laughed and shook his head. "You smoke too much, Humboldt," he said, "and you walk too little. You'll croak after all."

"Don't say things like that. Gimme a cigarette."

Yancy dropped his pack on the table. "This is Parker," he said, nodding his head toward Parker. "He's here for some equipment."

Humboldt said, "This the special order they told me about?" But he was too busy getting at one of Yancy's cigarettes to show much interest.

"This is him," Yancy said. He turned to Parker. "Last year," he said, "the doctor told Humboldt either he cut out the sauce or he'd be dead in six months. And I mean an important doctor, a doctor that knew his business, got his own column in the newspaper and been on TV and everything." He looked to Humboldt. "Isn't that right?"

Humboldt had the cigarette going now. "That doctor saved my life," he said.

"Yeah. We'll see." Back to Parker, Yancy said, "Humboldt hasn't had a drink since, not a taste. So he smokes instead, four five packs a day. And he eats, all the time. He put on seventy pounds so far, maybe more. Isn't that right, Humboldt?"

Humboldt said, "I'm alive, ain't I?"

"Sure you are." Yancy laughed and pulled one of the other chairs out from the card table and sat down. Motioning to Parker to take the third chair, at Humboldt's left, he said, "Humboldt don't walk any more, he weighs too much. He's tired all the time, and his mouth burns from all the weeds, and his stomach gives him a lot of trouble, but he's alive. That's the word he uses for it, alive. Isn't that right, Humboldt?"

Humboldt said, "I'm stayin' alive to give you pleasure, Yancy, that's the only reason." The cigarette stuck in the corner of his mouth, he seemed more at ease and with less of a whine in his voice.

The bartender came in then with a bottle and two glasses.

54

Humboldt shouted, "Get that garbage out of here!"

The bartender looked flustered. He said, "Yancy told me—"

"He wants to drink," Humboldt said, "he can go to the bar."

Yancy waved his arm, saying, "Humboldt, you're in a room full of the stuff. What's with you?"

"You and your booze get out of here, that's all."

Yancy shrugged and turned to Parker. "You need me right away?"

"No."

"Come on, Eddie."

Yancy and the bartender left. Humboldt said to Parker, "You want to go with him, come back when you're full?"

Parker said, "I'm here to buy guns."

In a different tone, Humboldt said, "You were with Yancy, I figured you were like him."

There was nothing to say to that. Parker waited.

Humboldt made a small gesture with his right hand, brushing something away. "You want guns," he said. "No drink, no cigarettes, no conversation, just guns."

There was still nothing to say.

Humboldt shook his head. "You and Yancy," he said. "Opposite sides of the same coin. What sort of guns you want?"

"Four handguns, any kind. Two machine guns. Four hand grenades."

"Hand grenades? They didn't say nothing about hand grenades."

Parker said, "You people hustle around too fast out here."

"What is that, sarcasm? You want hand grenades, I got to make a phone call."

Parker took one of Yancy's cigarettes and lit it. Humboldt looked at him, as though waiting for something, and then shook his head and pushed himself to his feet. He was a lot heavier than he'd looked sitting down; most of the weight had sagged below the waist, front and back. He said, "Come on along. They may want to talk to you."

Parker went with him, across the hall and into the office on the other side. This was a smaller room, full of office furniture. Humboldt sat at the desk and made his call. Parker leaned against the wall, ignoring the conversation, until Humboldt extended the phone toward him, saying, "He wants to talk to you."

Parker took it and said, "What is it?"

The voice was one he didn't recognize. It said, "What the hell you want with hand grenades?"

"What's your name?"

"Larris."

"Larris, you the guy sent Crystal to play games with me?"

"What's that got to do with hand grenades?"

Parker said, "Larris, you're a moron. You fuss around me once more, I let Karns know what a moron you are." Larris was trying to say something, but Parker wouldn't let him. He said, "I don't even want to be reminded of you, Larris. Now, listen. I'm going to explain something to you for the first and last time. Karns wants that island leveled. I'm not going to level it with my hands." He tossed the phone to Humboldt, who bobbled it but finally caught it, and leaned against the wall again.

Humboldt looked worried as he put the phone to his ear. "It's me, Mr. Larris," he said. "Humboldt." He talked some more, the whine strong in his voice, and Parker didn't listen.

When the conversation was done, Humboldt got heavily to his feet again and said, "Well, you get your hand grenades."

"I know."

"You," Humboldt said. "You're a hand grenade yourself."

They went back to the storeroom and Humboldt led the way down an aisle walled with cases of liquor. "Handguns," Humboldt said. At the end of the aisle he studied the labels on the cases for a minute, then tugged at one and the cardboard side opened like a flap, showing three quarts of Philadelphia whiskey and some cardboard dividers. "Rotten stuff," Humboldt said to himself, and took the three bottles out. He bent over with a grunt and put the bottles on the floor, then pulled out the cardboard dividers, and past the first row of three

56

bottles there weren't any bottles in the case at all. The interior had been lined with wood, to support the weight of the cases piled on top of it, and the hollow space was filled with smallish packages wrapped in rags.

Humboldt took one of the packages out, turned and turned it in his hands to unwind the rag, and inside was a revolver, a .32 Colt Detective Special with a two-inch barrel. He handed it to Parker, saying, "Used twice. No complaints."

It felt all right. The front sight had been taken off and identification marks had been filed away. It had a new smell to it and a solid feel, though a little small for Parker's hand.

The second gun Humboldt handed him was another of the same. "Used once," Humboldt said. The two guns were almost identical, though the removal of the front sight was a cleaner job on the first one.

Parker put these two on the floor, and Humboldt handed him a third, completely different from the first two. This was an automatic, a 9mm. Beretta Brigadier, much bigger than the Specials, heavier, a mean-looking machine. It was scratched up along the barrel and the grip was cracked in two places.

Parker said, "This one's no good."

"Don't you believe it," Humboldt said. "It's been used a dozen times out of here and everybody loves it. One kid, he asks for it every time, he's had it himself four times now."

Parker handed it back. "Save it for him," he said. "I'm not bringing these back."

"What? Nobody told me anything like that."

"Don't make any more phone calls," Parker said. "Larris won't like it."

Humboldt looked up at Parker's face. "It's your business," he said. He took the Beretta back, rolled it in its rag again, and stuffed it back into its cache. He fumbled around in there a minute, brought out another bundle, and this time unrolled another revolver, a five-shot S&W .38 Special Bodyguard, a hammerless model that could only be fired double-action. The rear of the gun, above the grip, had a naked hunchbacked look with its curve of plain metal where the hammer would be.

Parker said, "You want to get rid of this one."

"There's nothing wrong with it. We check them every time they come back, fire them, clean them. A bad gun doesn't go back in here."

Parker shrugged. The revolver looked all right. He put it on the floor with the other two.

Humboldt poked in the case a while and came out with a Colt .38 Super automatic. "This is a good one," he said. "This is a first-class good one."

Parker took it and it felt good. He turned his hand back and forth, holding the gun, and the weight was good, the feeling was good. "All right," he said. "That's four."

"Now you want two machine guns. Tommys I can't give you, but I got two Jugoslav-made Sten guns, they're old but they're reliable. You want to see them?"

"No. I'll take your word for it."

Humboldt smiled; that pleased him. He said, "Now, about hand grenades. That's what they call in the department stores a special order. When you gonna want this stuff?"

"Within a week."

"By Friday," said Humboldt. "That all right?"

Parker nodded. "Good."

"You want to take any of the stuff with you now, or get it all at once?"

"Leave it all together," Parker said. "I'll get word through Yancy where it should be delivered."

"That's good. Now, I don't expect to see any of this stuff again, is that right? Not even the Sten guns?"

"Nothing," Parker said.

Humboldt shrugged. "If that's the way it is, that's the way it is. Would you help me. . ."

He meant the liquor bottles. He didn't want to have to bend over for them. Parker picked them up and handed them to him, and Humboldt put everything back the way it was.

Walking back down the aisle, Parker in the lead, Humboldt

said, "You got to excuse me thinking you were like Yancy. You come in with him and all."

"Sure."

They got to the card table and Humboldt sat down with a sigh. He lit a fresh cigarette from Yancy's pack and put the rest of the pack in his pocket. He reached for the playing cards and started in on his solitaire game again.

Parker went out to the bar, where Yancy was draped. Yancy saw him coming and said, "There's my pal! Have a drink."

"Not now."

"You wanna go look at boats now?"

"No." The man who'd run the boat could pick one better than Parker.

Yancy said, "Well, it's time to go then." To the bartender he said, " Mind if I take the bottle, Eddie?"

"Just so you don't let no cop see you." The bartender explained to Parker, "All we're supposed to sell in here is set-ups."

Parker said to Yancy, "Give me the car keys."

"What? I can drive, don't you worry about me."

Parker snapped his fingers. "Give me the keys."

Yancy straightened up on his stool. Then he laughed and said, "Yes, sir," and handed Parker the keys to the Thunderbird. To the bartender he said, "This is the toughest buddy I got."

Parker went out to the car and Yancy trailed along behind him, bottle in one hand and glass in the other. They got into the car and pulled away, Parker making a U-turn and retracing the route to the Freeway.

When they were up on the Freeway and headed south, Yancy said, "You ever been in Houston before?"

"No."

"Then you done pretty good." Yancy poured a fresh drink. "When our work is all finished, you and I," he said, "we're going to have a nice long discussion about events and things."

Parker glanced at him. Yancy was smiling and cold-eyed.

Parker said, "When the job is done, I'll discuss anything you want, Yancy."

"Yeah," said Yancy. He nodded, slowly, continuously. "That's right," he said.

3

Grofield opened the door to Parker's knock. "Salsa's here," he said. "And a man to be our Charon."

"A what?"

"Someone to operate the boat."

"Oh." Parker went on into the living room where the other two men were.

Salsa got to his feet, smiling, his hand out. "Hello, Parker," he said. "Good to see you again."

"Hello, Salsa."

Salsa was a tall, slender, dark-haired man with gleaming white teeth, gleaming dark eyes, and the baby-face look of a gigolo. He'd been a gigolo once, and a professional revolutionary once, and a ballroom dancer once, and a lot of other things once. Now he said to Parker, "You're handling this job?"

"Yes."

"Then it's a good one."

Parker turned to the other man, a chunky beetling Irish type with dead white skin and dead black hair. Parker said, "You know boats?"

"Like I know how to breathe."

Parker turned and looked at Grofield. Grofield laughed and said, "He's a lyrical type, don't worry about it. He comes very highly recommended."

"By who?"

"Wymerpaugh."

"Yeah?" Parker turned back. "I'm Parker," he said.

"I presumed as much. The name's Heenan."

"What were you sent up for?"

Heenan blinked, and his mouth dropped open. "What's

that?"

"You haven't been out a week," Parker told him.

"How in God's name did you know that?"

"Boatmen are out in the sun a lot. They burn, they peel, they tan. Especially their foreheads. You're as white as a fish."

Heenan touched his hand to his forehead. "I'll burn," he said. "You're right, man, I'll burn like the condemned in Hell."

Parker said, "What were you up for?"

Heenan gestured with his hands, brushing things away. "A little problem," he said. "A minor peccadillo. I'm no longer afflicted."

"What was it?"

Heenan looked pained. He glanced at Grofield, at Salsa, back at Parker. He made a gesture as though to make unimportant what he was about to say, and he said, "It was what they call a sex offense."

"A sex offense."

"There was this girl they said wasn't eighteen, and in truth—"

"A sex offense," said Parker. "How old was she?"

Heenan cleared his throat. "Uhh, eleven."

Parker said, "How long were you in?"

"Five years, three months."

"Out of how much?"

"Fourteen years the judge gave me."

"So you're on parole. You reporting where you are, like they want?"

"Not me. Them big doors opened, I left."

Parker said. "Wait in the kitchen. I want to talk to these two guys."

Heenan said, "I'm cured of all that, I really am. There was a doctor at the prison, he—"

"I'm not looking for a baby-sitter," Parker told him. "You don't have to convince me."

"Oh. Yeah, sure. I'll, uh, I'll just go. . . ."

Heenan trailed away toward the kitchen, and when he was

gone Parker said, "That's the kind of guy blows a whole job wide open."

Salsa said, "I think we need somebody else." He had a quiet, polite, gentle voice and a manner to match.

Parker said to Grofield, "What did Wymerpaugh say about him?"

"I just asked for a boatman, Wymerpaugh says try Heenan. He didn't say anything about all this." Grofield seemed not only surprised but also insulted.

Salsa said, "He knows things now."

Parker frowned. "How much?"

Salsa checked it off: "Our names. That we're setting up a local operation and it needs a boat."

"That's all?"

Salsa looked a question at Grofield, and Grofield nodded. "That's all," he said. "We were leaving the orientation lecture up to you."

Parker said, "Then we can dust him with no trouble. Grofield, that's you."

"Because I brought him." Grofield sighed and shrugged his shoulders and said, "Right you are, as ever." He went on into the kitchen.

Salsa said, "Your woman got a telephone call, she had to go out. She said she'd be back early this evening."

Parker nodded. He wasn't thinking about Crystal, he was thinking about the job; they still had to find a boatman.

"Very good, that woman of yours," Salsa said, as he might have said something pleasant and admiring about a friend's new car. "She wishes to photograph me unclad."

Parker said, "We've got to find somebody. I'll call Handy McKay, maybe he knows somebody."

Grofield came out of the kitchen, leading Heenan. Grofield was an actor all the way through, and now he was playing the role of a cheerful amiable junior executive, giving to some lost nudnick the discreet bum's rush. "You see the position," he was saying, his arm draped over Heenan's shoulders. "No hard

63

feelings."

Heenan was looking confused and not yet sore. He'd get sore later, some time after Grofield finished sending him away.

Salsa said to Parker, "Would you mind?"

Parker watched Grofield and Heenan go by. Distracted, he said, "Mind? Mind what?"

"If I permit your woman to photograph me unclad."

Parker shook his head, not thinking about that. "What do I care?" he said. He went over to the telephone, and Grofield smilingly shut the door behind Heenan.

4

Parker rolled over, waking up, and the doorbell sounded again. Crystal was out; Grofield and Salsa were in the motel rooms being paid for by the Outfit. It was ten in the morning and Parker had been up till after three making his phone calls, waiting for answers, following leads and hints and suggestions, and still he had nobody to operate the boat.

He got up from the bed and stepped into his clothing and headed for the front door. The bell rang twice more in the time it took to dress and get there. He opened the door and it was a mistake.

Two guys outside had the flat broad look of Federal law. They were wearing dark suits with narrow lapels and dark hats with narrow brims. One of them carried a briefcase. They both had flat bony faces and expressionless eyes and prominent cheekbones. One of them said, "Speak to you, Mr. Parker," and they both bundled into the room.

Parker didn't like being at a disadvantage and these two had pushed into control from the outset. Pushing back was no good in this case; the way to get hold of the reins was pull in the direction they were pushing.

He shut the door after them and turned away, saying, "Making coffee. You can sit in the living room and wait."

"We'll come along with you."

"Sure. Come on."

They all went into the kitchen and he started water boiling for instant coffee. The other two sat at the kitchen table and while Parker got out the jar of coffee and three cups the guy with the briefcase said, in an easy, conversational tone of voice, "What is your real handle, Mr. Parker?"

"Parker, just like you said."

"Is it? Under the name Kasper, Arnold Kasper, you're wanted in California for the murder of a prison farm guard."

Parker said, "That's somebody else. How do you like your coffee?"

"Just black is fine for me. My partner takes a little sugar in his. You are also known as Charles Willis, and under that name you are wanted for two murders in Nebraska."

Parker said, "Wrong man. I never been in Nebraska." He put the cups and the sugar bowl and three spoons on the table.

"Under the name you claim as your own," the guy with the briefcase said, "you are alleged to have been involved in eight major robberies over the past eleven years. The number may be higher, of course, but eight we know about."

The other one said, "We don't seem to have a first name to go with Parker. Or is Parker the first name?"

Parker said, "You two are interested in names, you must have some of your own."

The one with the briefcase said, "Oh, I am sorry. I'm Mr. England and this is Mr. Carey."

Parker pointed at England and said, "Law." He pointed at Carey and said, "Accounting."

England smiled. "Very good, Mr. Parker," he said. "Bull'seye on both counts."

Carey said, "You should have hired Heenan."

Parker looked at him. "He was yours? Then I did right."

"No," said England. "If you had taken him on, Mr Parker, we would not have had to come and see you today. In fact, you would never have had occasion to see us at all."

The water was boiling. Parker turned the flame off and said, "This isn't a pinch."

"Not a bit of it," said England. "Murder and robbery do not interest us in the slightest."

"We're specialists," said Carey. "Those things are outside our specialty."

Parker poured water in the cups and then sat down at the table. "I could of left this room three times already," he said.

England said, "Why didn't you?"

"I want to know what's happening. What's your specialty?"

England said, "Baron von Altstein."

"Who?"

"Baron Wolfgang von Altstein."

Carey said, "You probably know the name Wolfgang Baron. Everybody's got extra names."

"The island," Parker said.

They both nodded. England said, "We want Von Altstein. We want him very very badly. I don't think you can imagine how badly we want him."

Parker said, "But he won't come in where you can grab him."

"No, he won't. It frustrates us."

Carey said, "We want him so bad, we'll take him instead of you."

Parker shook his head. "I don't follow."

England said, "We're onto the game, Mr. Parker. You've been asked to raid the Baron's island. You are currently assembling a group for just that objective."

"Wrong."

Carey said, "You deny everything, we know that, it's understood. Just let us say our say, all right?"

Parker said, "Fine. Tell your fairy tale."

"Here it is," said England. "You and your partners are going out to raid the island. You intend to come back with all the money you can lay your hands on. We want you to come back with the Baron, too."

"Do what?"

"We want the Baron," England said again. "You bring him in where we have jurisdiction and you'll have no problems. You won't be breaking any of our laws this time anyway."

"The helicopter," Parker said suddenly.

They both looked at him. Carey said, "What was that?"

Parker shook his head. "I've been trying to figure how you guys got in. It was that helicopter, the first time I went out to the island. You've been keeping a steady watch on the island, that's how you got onto me."

England seemed surprised. "Well, of course," he said. "How can we get the Baron if we don't watch the island he lives on?"

Parker said, "So what's Heenan got to do with it?"

"He was to have gone along, doing his assigned tasks in the robbery just as you would plan it, but in addition he would see to it that the Baron was brought in where we could get our hands on him."

Carey said, "It would simplify things if you'd reconsider hiring Heenan."

Parker shook his head. "He's no good."

"We know," said England apologetically, "but he was the best we could come up with on such short notice. We got him released from his jail term, you know."

Parked nodded. "He was too white to have been out a week, not down here."

Carey said, "The other choice is, you take me."

Parker looked at him. "I do what?"

"Bring me into the operation to do the job Heenan would have done. I'll do my part, and when it's all over I'll go my way with the Baron and you'll go your way with the loot."

Parker couldn't believe it. He said, "You're out of your mind."

"We mean it," Carey said.

England said, "It's one less man to split with, because Carey won't want any of the profits. Makes more for each of the rest of you."

"I'm supposed to tell the others about Carey?"

England frowned. Carey said, "It probably would be best if you didn't. It's up to you."

"You two," Parker told them, "are just bright enough to do stupid things with smart details."

Carey said, "You're talking like a man with a choice."

"I've always got a choice."

"No. Not this time."

"Show me."

It was England who answered. "We want the Baron, as we said, badly enough to let you go in trade. But if we don't get him we'll take you as a consolation prize. It's as simple as that."

"We could have had you," Carey said, "any time in the last few days."

"Either time you went out to the island, for instance," England said. "Or when you went to the Tropical Palm Lounge in Houston to arrange for guns. You're a better driver than Yancy, by the way."

"We have the manpower," Carey said, "and we have the interest. We've had you in sight from the beginning; we could have picked you up any time. We still can."

"If you refuse to help us," England said, "or if you try to leave the area without going through with the robbery, we will pick you up."

Parker said, "Drink your coffee. Let me think."

England shrugged. "Go right ahead."

Parker got to his feet, went over to the kitchen sink, turned the cold water on, and doused water over his face and head. He dried off with paper towels, then went through the cabinets over the sink until he found a can of mixed nuts. He sat back down at the table, drank his coffee, ate handfuls of the mixed nuts, and thought it out.

The alternatives were three: Clear out of here right now. Go along with Carey and England all the way. Work some sort of compromise.

His instinct hold him to go for number one. England and Carey were sloppy, because they were sure of themselves. He could overpower them any time, then look the situation over and find a way out of the building past the reserve troops that were bound to be outside. Go north and east, get far away from this part of the country and lie low for a while.

The main thing wrong with that, he wouldn't be able to alert Grofield and Salsa, so the law would naturally take them as a consolation prize for him.

So maybe a combination of one and two. Promise to go along

with Carey and England, then get the word to Grofield and Salsa, and the three of them wait for a good time to clear out of here.

Which wasn't good either. Most of the time, a lone man can break free of surveillance if he wants to badly enough and if he has some experience, but with three men trying it all at once the odds are too high, at least one of them will get grabbed.

Besides that, Parker was in this operation because he needed the money. His cut would be forty thousand, guaranteed, and forty thousand would give him the cushion he needed right now. If there was any safe way to keep the operation alive, he'd do it.

Then maybe alternative number two; go along with Carey and England all the way. Except that Carey and England were stupid. Trying to get a bad risk like Heenan in on the job, and now even trying to get one of themselves in with him. As though this weren't a profession, as though a job like this didn't need personnel who knew their business and could be counted on no matter which way things went. It was obvious Carey and England had no understanding of Parker's line of work, and that meant, if he did go through with the job, he'd have to keep control of it out of their hands.

Which came to alternative number three, the compromise. Work out an arrangement with Carey and England that would get them what they wanted and him what he wanted. It was possible they could come to some sort of middle ground even though neither of them trusted the other. Carey and England mistrusted Parker because he was outside the law, and Parker mistrusted them because he was convinced at the end of everything they'd be trying for Baron and himself both. If they could put the arm on him, they'd be crazy to let the chance go by, and he didn't think they were crazy.

Finally he said, "All right. A proposition."

Carey said, "I don't think you're in a position to bargain."

Parker told him, "I'm looking to see if I can get an arrangement where it would be safer for me to stay with this job than to try to make a break for it right now. The way you two are handling it, it's safer for me to make the break."

England held a hand up, saying, "All right, we'll listen. We're reasonable men."

Carey glanced at his partner, but he didn't say anything more.

Parker said, "What you want is Baron. You don't care how you get him, so the details don't—"

"We want him alive," England said hastily. "Don't get us wrong, we won't be satisfied with proof of his death or anything like that. We want Von Altstein very much alive."

"There's a trial waiting for him," Carey said. "A big public trail, and a rope at the other end of it."

"I don't care," Parker said. "You want him alive, that's all you care about. The Baron, or Von Altstein, or whatever you call him, you want him in on dry land where you've got jurisdiction. So I'll go along with you, I'll bring him in for you. But that's all of it. I don't have any law or any pigeons working with me. You people leave me strictly alone to do my own job my own way, and when my job is done you'll get your piece of it."

They looked at each other, both of them doubtful. England said, "What sort of guarantee—"

"No guarantee. You say you've got me in a bind, you're watching me so close with so many troops I can't get away from you no matter what. So you guarantee the job yourself."

Carey said, "We could consider it."

"You mean you want to check with somebody higher up. Use the phone in the bedroom, it's quicker that way."

They looked at each other again, and then England nodded and said, "I'll go. I won't be long."

Parker said to Carey, "You want more coffee?"

Carey watched England leave the room, then turned to Parker. "No, thanks."

"I do." Parker went over by the sink again, opened cupboards, closed them, opened drawers, closed them, palmed a steak knife and went back over to the table. Suddenly his left hand had a grip on Carey's hair and his right hand was holding the knife to Carey's throat. "Don't move," he whispered.

Carey wasn't that stupid. He stayed where he was; only his eyes had widened a little.

Parker let go his hair and used that hand to frisk Carey, finding his revolver, a businesslike S&W .38 Special, in a belt holster on his right hip. Parker backed away, holding the revolver, and put the steak knife back in its drawer. He faced Carey, keeping the revolver where Carey could see it without its being exactly aimed anywhere in particular.

Parker said, "England comes back in here, I disarm him. That's easy. The three of us go out, we flag a cab. None of your troops follows because there's two of you and one of me so they figure I'm well covered. Then blocks away I shoot you and England and the cabby, drive the cab to Houston, take a plane. Any problems?"

Carey said nothing.

Parker walked back across the room and put the revolver down on the table. "That's your guarantee," he said. "I could do that, and I won't. I need this operation, and if you and your friends don't screw it up I'll run it off as scheduled."

Carey picked up his revolver, looked at it a second, then put it away. His voice mild, distracted, he said, "I'm not a specialist in people like you."

"You're lucky," Parker told him.

Carey studied Parker as though making up his mind whether or not to buy him. "Maybe I will," he said. "When this is over, when we've got Von Altstein and you go off your own way, maybe I'll put in for a transfer. Maybe we'll meet each other again some other time."

Parker doubted it, but he knew why Carey was saying it. It was a way to get some of his pride back. So Parker just shrugged and sat down at the table and said, "Maybe so."

England came back a couple minutes later. "They want some sort of assurance," he said.

Carey said, "It's all right. We've got the assurance."

"We do?"

"Mr. Parker just took my gun away, held it on me, and explained exactly how he could kill the two of us and a passing cabdriver and get himself out of this situation, if he wished to do so. It was plausible, particularly with him holding my gun on me while he explained it all."

England was frowning, looking back and forth at the two of them. He said, "Then what?"

"Then he gave the gun back to me," Carey said.

England said, "I don't get it."

"I do," Carey said. He got to his feet. "It's all yours, Mr. Parker," he said. "You won't see us again till you come back to shore with Von Altstein."

Not even then, Parker thought. Aloud, he said, "I'll see you then."

5

"If the deal is queer," said Grofield, "it's queer. I say we get the hell out while the getting is good."

"Anything they'll make on you," Parker told him, "they've already made. From now till the job's done they'll keep their distance."

Salsa said, "What about after the job?"

"It's a big coastline."

The fourth man in the room, Ross, said, "Up to now they haven't made me at all, is that right?"

Parker nodded. "That's right."

Ross was the boatman; Salsa had turned him up. He was big, stocky, florid, with heavy pale eyebrows and thick pale hair and thick freckled hands. He said, "I could leave this building right now, the same way I came in, just as careful, and they'd never make me at all."

"That's right."

"But if I stay, it's fifty thousand dollars guaranteed minimum."

"That's right."

"If I stay," Ross deliberately, "I'll be very careful they never do make me."

Parker nodded. "That's sensible."

"Even if it complicates the work," Ross said. "I want you to know that. This adds another element, this makes the situation tricky. If I agree to do something, and then it turns out I can't do that something without tipping my mitt to your friends, you're just gonna have to count me out."

"I already figured that," Parker told him.

Ross said, "I just wanted to make it clear."

Grofield said, "Parker, I've never seen you anything but

cautious. How come you're still in this? The job is tipped to the Federal law, why aren't we all the hell out of here?"

Parker told him, "About this job, this island thing, from a law standpoint they don't give a damn. It's not their jurisdiction, not their fight. That island is Cuban territory, so it's up to the Cuban cops to get after us, and right now the Cuban cops and American cops don't get along too good. About anything else, anything they might have on me or you from the past, they aren't interested because it isn't their department."

Grofield said, "They can send an interoffice memo."

Parker nodded. "I know that. That's why we say we'll play along but when the job is done we find some other piece of coast to land at."

Grofield said, "They've got helicopters, they've got a whole goddam Navy, not to mention the Coast Guard and the Air Force. Why should they let us go there and come back without them watching?"

Parker said, "No reason. They'll be tailing us the best they can."

"It'll be a pretty good best."

"Not good enough. It'll be at night, and the island will be going up in flames, and there'll be thirty boats heading away from there at once, maybe more, all Baron's customers getting the hell out. The Federals know we mean to knock over the island, but they don't know we mean to knock it all the way out, and that's our edge."

"I like wide edges," Grofield said. "That one looks narrow to me."

"If you're in," Parker told him, "we'll talk about it. If you're out, what difference does it make?"

Grofield frowned, thinking about it. He said, "Salsa, what about you? You still in this?"

Salsa said, "I think about it. What do they have now, so far? My name. My fingerprints, I suppose, from something in the motel. But they don't have me, and they won't come to get me till after this job. So what do I care? Police have had my name, my fingerprints, a hell of a long time. They'll be looking for me after this job, but once more what do I care, they've been looking for me already half a dozen years."

Grofield said, "They've been tapping our phones. That's the only way they could have known I'd be trying to get in touch with Heenan. They heard me talk to Wymerpaugh, heard him say Heenan. They checked Heenan fast, found him in stir already, put a band on his leg and sent him to us."

Parker said, "We've got to find safe phones, call back everybody we called before, tell them what's up so they can protect themselves."

Ross said, "What about this bird Heenan?"

"I already called Wymerpaugh," Parker said. "He'll take care of that."

Grofield said, "If we can widen that edge, make it surer we'll get out from under any watch they'll have on us, then I'm still in."

Salsa said, "One thing we could do." When they all looked at him, he said, "Every night we lose our shadows. Right after dark every night. We get new places to stay at night, and we don't come back where they can pick us up again until the morning."

Grofield said, "What good does that do?"

"We do it five, maybe six nights," Salsa told him. "The fifth night, the sixth night, we go out to the island. Every night they have to guess we are going to the island, and they watch the island. Night after night. The fifth night, maybe the sixth night, they're getting a little careless. Could be we get there and start the fuss before they even know it, catch them by surprise. They don't know when we got there, how we got there, so they don't know when or how we'll leave."

"Easier than that," Parker said. "You and Grofield go out there every night. On the job, you'll be going out in Baron's boat anyway, so you do it every night. I disappear. They know the job's still on because you two are around, but they can't find me. Every night for a week you two go out to the island, eat a meal, lose a little dough we'll get from the Outfit, come back. Then one night Ross and I go out and we do the job. They don't know how we got there, they never even see Ross, and we're away free and clear."

Ross said, "I don't want them seeing me at the end of it all, going back to the mainland."

Parker told him, "They can see you and not connect you with us. We can work that out."

"How?"

Grofield said, "What if we hire some people, a few boys and girls to be like a party? Ross takes them out to the island, they keep out of the way while we're working, and then they stand around on deck while Ross takes us all back to the mainland. We three stay down below."

Ross nodded, saying, "That could work. You'd all have to be careful you weren't seen coming to the boat, that's all."

"We don't have to hire anybody," Parker said. "There'll be more people than boats out there. We just move some of the extra down to our boat, people who didn't come in boats of their own."

"And where do we hit land?" Ross asked. "Not back to Galveston."

"No city at all," Parker told him. "Just a beach, someplace like that. You and I, we pick the place beforehand, put a car there to be ready for us."

Grofield said, "And our passengers?"

"What about them?"

Grofield shrugged. "What do we do with them, once we land and it isn't Galveston?"

"We leave them," Parker said. "We get in the car and go. What's the problem?"

"Just asking," said Grofield.

Salsa said, "We still do it, then. The same as before, the same as we worked out, but with these extras."

Parker said, "There's no reason to walk out on it."

"Good luck to us," said Grofield. "Bonne chance to us.

Parker, you get very funny jobs. Copper Canyon was only slightly crazy compared to this. This time, the law knows the job is going to be pulled, knows who's going to do it and how, and doesn't care. It's like walking into a bank and the guard at the door hands you a piece of paper and on it is the combination to the vault."

Ross got to his feet. "If we're done. . ."

They were done. Parker said to him, "I'll be in touch with you tomorrow, after I shake my tail."

"Good. I'd like to leave first, boys, if it's all right."

Grofield said, "Sure. We'll give you five minutes."

After Ross left, Salsa said, "How many days?"

"Eight. We'll hit at ten forty-five the eighth night." Parker got to his feet. "Wait a second." He went back to the bedroom, where Crystal was waiting for them to be finished, and said, "Come in here a minute."

"Sure thing." She'd been lying in bed, reading, wearing an orange sweater and black stretch pants. She got up and stepped into shoes and followed him into the living room.

Parker said, "From now on, the contact with the Outfit is through Grofield and Crystal. Grofield's going to want some stuff, some money and maybe other things, and he'll talk through you. Right?"

Crystal smiled at Grofield. "I don't care," she said.

"I don't mind myself," Grofield told her.

Salsa got to his feet. "Time for us to leave. See you soon, Parker."

Grofield and Salsa headed for the door, Grofield saying to Crystal, "I may need lots of stuff. All kinds of stuff."

"You just come and talk to me," she said.

"Count on it, honey."

They left, and Parker went to the bedroom to pack. Crystal came after him and stood in the doorway saying, "You going away?"

"Got to. Part of it."

"You have to leave this minute? It couldn't wait half an

hour?"

He barely listened to her, didn't get what she meant. His thoughts now were limited to the job. He said, "Now's the best time," and finished packing. She sulked when he left, but it was wasted; he never saw it.

THREE

1

Grofield walked into the department store, took an elevator up to the second floor and the stairs back down, left through a different door to a different street, flagged a cab and rode three blocks, then jumped from the cab into a city bus.

Straphanging in the bus, Grofield considered. Should he lose the third one, too? Then let them find him again back at the motel.

There was no point in any of this, it was just Grofield's way to fill the dull spaces. Eight days of inactivity were stretching out like a rubber band toward the robbery at the far end, and Grofield had stood three days of it before going dramatic. Men like Parker and Salsa could just sit there, silent and patient, waiting for the moment to go to work, but Grofield wasn't built like that.

There was an air of dark energy around Grofield, a nervous predatory pacing. He wasn't a man who liked to be still. In his acting work he was most often cast as a heavy, either a villain or some sort of sick weakling, and he himself was proudest of his performance as Iago, a lean and sensual and catlike Iago, in a tent theater production of *Othello* in Racine, Wisconsin. Had he gone to Hollywood he would have made his fortune in television, and he knew it, but television was not for him. He was dedicated, sincere, juvenile; only the legitimate theater was worth the expenditure of true acting talent.

There's a good living in the legitimate theater for a very few, and a rotten living for a great multitude. Never having made it big, and being so weighed down with acting integrity it was unlikesalsly he ever would make it big, Grofield was a member of acting's underpaid multitude. But his other profession — the vocation he practiced every year or so with men like Parker and

Salsa and Ross — supported him just fine, made it possible for him to remain an actor, keep his integrity, and still live as well as he wanted.

The two professions complemented one another. The robberies helped him in his characterizations of the roles he was so often given to play, and the acting ability more than once had come in handy in the course of a robbery. Both professions appealed to the same urgent, dramatic, energetic streak in him, and in spending his time between them Grofield was a happy man.

Except for inactivity. He couldn't stand to have nothing to do. to be forced to wait.

This time, he had lasted three days. Each evening he and Salsa went out to the island, had dinner, watched the cockfights, gambled a little, and finally came back to shore; that time was pleasant, bearing a kind of muted drama. But the mornings and afternoons were just empty, and emptiness was what Grofield couldn't stand. For three days he'd filled the dead hours as best he could with movies, but by now he'd seen every movie in the Galveston area he wanted to see, and a few he didn't want to see, and so today there was nothing for it but to play games.

It had taken him an hour of erratic, pulsing, random motion around Galveston and Texas City and LaMarque before he had been sure how many Federals were following him and what each of them looked like. Another half hour of prowling, starting and stopping, hurrying and creeping, turning and back-tracking, had made him familiar with their methods. Now, in five minutes of razzle-dazzle, he'd cut them from three to one, and he knew he could get rid of the third any time he wanted. The question was, did he want?

Reluctantly, he decided he'd better not. Already Parker had dusted them off his tail; if now Grofield did the same thing, they might not wait around for him to show back at the motel. They might grab Salsa right away, seeing as Salsa would be all they'd have left. They might just louse up the whole operation if Grofield played too many games with them.

Grofield shrugged. At the next stop, he swung down off the bus and walked back to the cab parked half a block away. The Fed was playing it as cagey as possible under the circumstances, staying in the cab until he saw exactly what Grofield was going to do next.

Grofield strolled back and stuck his head in the cab window. "I'm going back to the motel now," he said pleasantly. "Why don't we take the same cab and save us some money?"

The Fed looked at him with disgust. Federal agents were all alike; upright, honest, courteous, kind, self-righteous, and humorless. "Take your own cab," he said.

"You're wasting the taxpayers' money," Grofield told him.

The Fed didn't say anything. He turned his head and looked stonily out the other window. Up front the cabby was grinning and trying not to show it.

"Have it your own way," Grofield said. "I'll see you later." He straightened up and started away, then changed his mind and went back, saying, "Correction, I'm not going back to the motel. I'm going first to see the fair Crystal, and *then* I'm going back to the motel."

The Fed turned and looked at Grofield. "I have patience," he said. "I have patience and I can wait."

Grofield grinned at him. "You remind me of Parker," he said. "The two of you, sparkling, scintillating, a million laughs." He waved, and went away again, and this time flagged a cab and rode it to Crystal's apartment house.

He had an excuse for going, if not exactly a reason. Crystal was his contact with the Outfit, from whom all blessings flowed, including the money Grofield and Salsa were spending every night out on the island of Cockaigne, and it was more or less true they needed more cash. They had enough to last another couple of days, so he was rushing things a little going to see Crystal now, but he felt up, he felt tense and expectant, the little bit of horseplay with the Federal agents had only whetted his appetite for more.

The other cab trailed along like something attached by a

string. Grofield looked back at it from time to time and laughed, picturing the Parker-like face of that Federal man back there. When he got out of the cab at Crystal's place he paused long enough to wave at the Fed before going on into the building.

Grofield heard music, movie-type background music. He heard it all the time, in every part of his life. For the last half hour or so the music had all been of cops-and-robbers movie type, with a lot of drums and trumpets and syncopation, but now as he went up in the elevator to Crystal's apartment the music changed, became light, frothy, semicomic, the kind of music that backs Jack Lemmon or Cary Grant on their way to see Shirley MacLaine or Doris Day. Grofield strode out of the elevator whistling and did a little dance step in the middle of the hall.

At first, after he rang the bell, he thought she wasn't home. He waited and waited by the closed door, while the music began to change again, and soon the air around his head was swollen with tear-stained violins; missing in action, erroneously reported dead, he was returning home at last, shattered in mind and body, five years after the war, not yet knowing his wife had remarried.

But the n the door opened and she was standing there in a robe, not entirely awake. Sleepiness didn't bloat Crystal, as it does to so many, it merely made her a bit fuzzy around the edges. She said, "Wha? What is it?"

"It's two p.m., my darling. Forgive my waking you so early, but I didn't want you to miss the sunset."

"I was taking a nap. You want to come in?"

"Sweetheart, you don't know how I've longed to hear those words from your lips."

She squinted, trying to bring his face and her mind both into focus. Her robe was half open, and underneath it she was wearing pale blue pajamas. "You're kidding around," she said.

"That's right," he said, "I am. Do you want to sleep some more? I'll come back later."

"No, no, that's all right. Come on in."

86

She stepped out of the way and Grofield walked into the apartment, shutting the door behind him. They both went into the living room, and she said, "You want a cup of coffee or something?"

"Coffee? I didn't just get up, you did. I'll take the something."

She waved a hand vaguely. "Bar's over there. Excuse me, I'll be back in just a minute."

"Don't get dressed," he said.

She squinted some more. She was one of the few women Grofield had ever met who could squint without ruining her looks. She said, "What was that?"

"You look very sexy," he said. "Robe and pajamas, very sexy. If you just had the robe on, half open like that, that would be just conventionally sexy, you know what I mean? But with the blue pajamas, just the hint of an outline of breast, swell of hip, it adds a whole new dimension."

She was waking up now. "Is that right?" she said, and her tone said tell-me-more.

Grofield said, "I've noticed the same thing about my wife."

"You're married?"

"Yes."

She nodded thoughtfully. "You start a pass," she said, "and then you tell me you're married. Now you go back to throwing the pass, right?"

Grofield grinned and nodded. "Right."

"And if I take you up on it, it's on your terms. I already know you're married, so I can't have any complaints later on."

"If it was a line I'd worked up, honey," he said, "I would have used it before I was married and today I might not *be* married."

"If you are."

"Oh, I am, all right."

She seemed to consider, and then she said, "If I'm going to be catching passes, I ought to have something to drink. But I just woke up."

"Coffee royal."

"I was thinking the same thing. Wait here, I'll go make the coffee."

Grofield smiled after her as she left the room. Easiest thing in the world, and a nice pleasant way to fill the mornings and afternoons between now and work time. A lot more fun than tantalizing Feds, too.

Parker was crazy, moving out on something like this.

She came back eventually, with two cups of black coffee on a tray. She set it down on the coffee table and went over to the bar, saying, "I don't understand you guys, and I've met a million of you."

Grofield didn't believe there were a million of him. He said, "Such as?"

"Married, but on the prowl. If you're gonna keep going back to the wife, why leave her? If you're going to keep leaving her, why go back?"

"Two different things," Grofield told her, thinking he ought to call Mary today. He'd do it when he left here.

"Two different things," echoed Crystal. "I don't get it." She came over with a bottle of whiskey. "Where's your wife now? In town here?"

"Good God, no. In Estes Park, Colorado."

"Is that where you live? How much of this stuff should we pour in?"

"As much as the cup will hold, my dear. Very nice. No, she is acting with a theatrical troupe. As will I be in few weeks."

Interest quickened in her eyes. "You're an actor?"

"The heir apparent to the crown of John Barrymore, that's all."

"What have you been—?"

But the doorbell sounded, breaking into the question, leaving Grofield with mixed emotions. He was glad the trite question had been interrupted, but irritated to have the progression with this delightful girl interrupted. He said, "Ignore it."

"I can't. It might be something important." She was already

on her feet and halfway across the room.

"Ah, well. Hurry back to me."

She flashed him a smile over her shoulder and went on out to the foyer. A minute later she was back, looking troubled, and behind her came two men, one of them the Fed who earlier had refused to share a cab with Grofield. He was the one who said, "Alan Grofield?"

"You have the honor," Grofield told him.

Crystal said, "Is that your first name? Alan? I like that."

"Nice of you."

"You come with us," said the Fed, talking to Grofield.

Something cold touched Grofield in the pit of the stomach. "This is a pinch?"

The other Fed said, "You're not under arrest, don't worry about it. We want to talk to you."

"Why don't we talk here? Sure lovely surroundings, a charming hostess. . ."

"Downtown," said the first Fed.

"You," Grofield told him, "are trying to be difficult. And are succeeding wondrous well. All right, if you insist you insist." He got to his feet and said to Crystal, "I'll come back when I can. We'll continue our discussion.'"

"I'll like that."

Grofield smiled at her, a trifle sadly — Rex Harrison as the gentle jewel thief, being taken from the hotel suite in Cannes — and patted her cheek as he went by. The background music was ironic, sophisticated, subtly jazzy.

Riding down in the elevator, down a corridor, and into an office where a middle-aged white-haired gent who looked like Hopalong Cassidy said, "Sit down, Mr. Grofield."

Grofield sat down. "I won't tell who Mister Big is," he announced. "My lips are sealed."

Hopalong Cassidy rewarded him with a thin smile. " We know *who* Mister Big is," he said. "What we want to know is *where* he is. Where's Parker?"

Grofield did Willy Best, big eyes and sagging underlip and

all. "Who? Who dat?"

Hopalong Cassidy shook his head, but was still smiling around the corners of his mouth. "Don't play like that, Mr. Grofield," he said. "If you won't talk sense with me, I'll just have to have you detained for a day or two until you feel more reasonable."

Grofield shook his head. "No, you won't. You detain me and everybody else runs out and the whole deal is off. You know that as well as I do."

"They'd leave you?" Hopalong acted as though he thought he could get mileage out of that idea.

Grofield nipped it in the bud. "They'd leave me," he said, "almost as fast as I'd leave them."

Hopalong leaned back in his chair and tapped some fingers on his desk. "We want to know what's going on," he said. "We want to know where Parker is, and we want to know when you people are going out to that island."

"We go out there every night."

"You know what I mean, Grofield."

Grofield was suddenly bored. He shook his head. "Parker's doing some of the groundwork," he said. "I don't know where he is because it doesn't matter where he is. When he's got things set he'll get in touch with me, and a few days after that we'll do the job."

"Why did Parker lose our men?"

"No, no, it's the other way around. You want to know why your men lost Parker."

"Parker deliberately shook them."

"Maybe for fun, the same as me this afternoon. I shook two of them, and I could have got rid of the third one too."

The third one was one of the two Feds standing over by the door. He cleared his throat and said, "Don't be so sure of yourself, you."

Grofield smiled at Hopalong Cassidy. "Shall we have a dry run? Use all the men you want, in one hour I'll be clear. Little side bet to add spice?"

90

Hopalong shook his head. "I don't understand you people," he said. "You don't make sense. You do this, you do that, but nothing happens."

"We're subjects of the red queen," Grofield told him, knowing he wouldn't get it and not giving a damn.

Hopalong waved a hand as though he were tired of Grofield, disgusted with Grofield, uninterested in Grofield. "Go on," he said. "Go on about your business."

"Bless you." Grofield, smiling, got to his feet. To the two at the door he said, "Come along, chums. We have unfinished business in a lady's apartment."

2

Baron Wolfgang Friedrich Kastelbern von Altstein lay on his back on a maroon carpet and raised his bare right leg perpendicular to the floor. He lowered it again and raised the left leg. Then the right leg. Then the left leg. Across the way, Steuber sat morose in a red-upholstered Victorian chair, his watch in one hand and an exercise book in the other. He counted aloud as Baron — he called himself, these days, Wolfgang Baron — raised each leg, and when he reached thirty Baron rolled over on his face and started doing push-ups.

Steuber looked at his watch. "Forty-five seconds ahead," he said.

Baron grunted and kept on with the push-ups.

He was fifty-seven years old now, but no one would guess he was much over forty. He kept himself in good physical and mental shape at all times. Doing push-ups now, dressed in white T-shirt and black bathing trunks, he looked the picture of health, a man with thirty or forty years of life left in him.

His life had started, in Kiel, Germany, just a few years before the First World War. His father, the fourth Baron, was at that time a major in the German army, a Prussian career officer like his own father and his father's father. By the time the war had nearly run its course he was a general, and then just a few months later he was a civilian. By 1920, bewildered by a world that seemed to have no use for any of his barbaric arts, he was dead in his own bed and his son Wolfgang had inherited his title, his old uniforms, and his debts.

Baron grew up in a Germany of chaos. He was too young to be part of the *Freikorps*, battling the undeclared war on the Polish frontier in the early twenties, but he turned eighteen and graduated from the gymnasium just in time to be swept into the maw of National Socialism, the new movement that was already being called by the slang word Nazi. He was living in Danzig then, with an uncle on his mother's side, and every Sunday he could be found in the big park wearing his brown uniform, singing the marching songs, and listening to the speeches. The SA was a good place for a young man in the late twenties. Comradeship, good drinking parties, singing and marching, carousing, truck rides in the country, now and then a good brawl with the Poles or with some other political bunch. Baron was pleased to be in the SA, and the SA was just as pleased to have him; some day he might prove useful, what with his hereditary army connections. The army at that time had not yet been brought within the Nazi sphere.

After Hitler's takeover and the capitulation of the army, it was suggested to Baron that he leave the SA and accept an army commission, but he was still youthful at heart and preferred to stay with the crowd he knew. It was only with the murder of Roehm and the near-downfall of the SA organization completely that he decided to move on, and then it was not to the army that he went but to the SS. The army had killed his father by becoming all-important to him and then deserting him. The army would have no such chance with the son.

The war, when it arrived, matured Baron and taught him things about himself he'd never guessed were there. He was already in his thirties, but still acted like a college kid on a spree, until the war came along.

The first thing he learned about himself was that he was afraid to die. Men could fight for the Fatherland anywhere in the world they wanted, but they'd fight without Baron. It wasn't patriotism that had stirred him at the rallies all these years but merely pageantry, and it wasn't the Fatherland that had lifted his heart but merely the Fatherland's beer.

The second thing he learned about himself was that he was a natural opportunist, with innate skill and native balance. In a world gone mad, self-interest approaches the level of a sacrament, so it was with a will that Baron launched himself into his new-found vocation: Looking Out for Number One. (He had a little joke in those days, used only when among his closest and dearest friends. "I hate to be chauvinistic, but. . ." and then finish the sentence with something viciously anti-Nazi or anti-Hitler or anti-Germany or possibly just pro-Baron.)

His activities during the war were varied, lucrative, and extremely safe. He entered France well behind the combat troops — three months behind — and became one of the overseers in the plunder of French art treasures, most of which was shipped to Germany but some of which Baron siphoned away for his own use at another time when the world should roll over once again. Later he was an administrative part of the famous scheme to flood Great Britain with bogus pound notes, and a few cartons of the counterfeits very quietly disappeared to a cache that only Baron knew.

Although almost everything he engaged in during the Second World War was a crime, none of it — he was always a careful man — came under the heading of war crime, so the name Wolfgang von Altstein appeared on no one's list of most-wanted Germans. The war's end found him in Munich, in hastily assembled civilian clothing and armed with the false set of identity papers he'd had made up two years before for just such an emergency. On these identity papers the name Wolfgang Baron first appeared. The papers claimed Baron had been a language teacher at a school in Berlin — he did speak English, French, and Spanish, all fluently — and that his sole connection with the Nazi Party or any German military organization was his membership in the *Volkssturm,* the home guard of the old, the very young, and the lame, assembled from the remnants of German maledom toward the end of the war.

With the coming of peace, Baron traded his black uniform for the black market, exchanging watches and cameras for coffee and gasoline and cigarettes. This interim activity kept him going and earned him some pleasant profit until 1948, when it was possible for him to move abroad and begin converting various of his acquisitions to cash.

94

He lived in France for the next eight years, slowly selling off the art works he'd commandeered during the war, and it was his expectation to live the rest of his life in France, well off and well out of trouble.

But then the roof fell in. The biggest Nazis had long since been taken care of, and the lesser Nazis were almost all either dead or captured. Smaller and smaller fish were added to the lists of wanted men, simply because the lists gave so many men in so many countries a source of livelihood, and in the late fifties the name of Baron Wolfgang Friedrich Kastelbern von Altstein made the grade. Charge: war crimes. Specifics: the looting of France. Some enlisted men, truckdrivers and such, had ratted on him.

He found out in time to get out from under, but not in time to liquidate all his assets. He landed in Spain still a wealthy man, but with his wealth cut just about in half and with his opportunities for accumulating more money drastically diminished. He lived for several years in Spain, living on his capital, and when he was approached by the Russians for potential espionage work he was more than willing to take their money. Unfortunately the deal fell through before he made a pfennig; the truth was, he didn't know anything the Russians could use and he didn't know any way to find out anything the Russians could use. Espionage had never been a part of his world.

Still, this contact with the Russians proved fruitful a couple of years later, when he decided to move on, establish himself in a country more productive of opportunities for money-making than Spain, and made the mistake of first choosing the United States.

He never did find out how they'd gotten onto him. He had established himself in New Orleans, being part owner of various night clubs and motels, and suddenly he was in the middle of a covey of Federal agents. He ran like a hare, and if it hadn't been for the reserve fund he had prudently salted away in a Swiss bank he would have left the United States penniless.

As it was, he was far from rich. He took immediate refuge in Cuba, the one place in the western hemisphere he was sure American policemen could not enter in search of him, and established his identity by mentioning the names of the two Russians with whom he had had dealings in Madrid a few years before. He claimed now to have contacts within the United States, and promised to create an espionage apparatus for the Russians if he was given their cooperation. No money, he assured them, not until and unless he delivered. All he asked was their nonfinancial support in his establishing himself. If thereafter he failed to produce anything worthwhile, the Russians would not have lost a thing.

They agreed, as a speculative venture. Baron had known for twenty years of the nameless nationless unwanted island off the Texas coast; there had been foolish talk at one point during the war about establishing a fueling base for U-boats there. He arranged for Cuba to claim the island — it was nearly nine hundred miles from Cuba, but the Azores were over two thousand miles from Portugal and the world is full of similar precedents, so no serious objections were raised, except in the United States House of Representatives, which fulminated about "takeovers" but which couldn't do a damn thing about it — and he himself named the place Cockaigne, an ironic reference to the land of idleness and luxury in the old legends. It was easy to convince the Russian intelligence officers that a gambling island off the American coast was a good base for espionage, and if the results of the espionage were slow in coming it was still true that Baron had cost the Russians nothing but a little wasted anticipation.

Now he had the island and the casino, and life was pleasant. He had no espionage apparatus, and no intention to establish one, and because he knew how often and how rapidly the world turned over and the politicians and intelligence officers were reshuffled and redealt, he wasn't particularly worried. He could stall the Russians until new alignments should make their current hopes for him obsolescent.

And now, as ever, the most important thing was to keep himself alive, and healthy, and financially secure, and as safe as possible from his enemies. For this he had the island and the casino and the exercises and Steuber.

Steuber had been with him since 1939, in Berlin. At that time, at the beginning, he had been Baron's chauffeur. In the years since he had been Baron's butler, valet, bodyguard, go-between, whipping boy, and confidant. He was Baron's army, Baron's family, Baron's circle of friends. In ways that neither of them clearly understood, Steuber was Baron's world and equally so was Baron the world for Steuber.

"Forty," said Steuber now, and peered at the stopwatch. "Twenty-five seconds ahead."

Baron rested a few seconds on the floor after his fortieth push-up, then hoisted himself to his feet and started running in place. Steuber counted each time Baron's right foot touched the floor. Baron ran with fists clenched, head up, eyes staring straight ahead. Running, he looked like a fanatic.

At first neither of them heard the knocking at the door, but when Baron did notice it he turned his head and glared in that direction, because the staff knew he was not to be disturbed while exercising. But the knocking wouldn't stop, so Baron took over the counting himself, without losing the pace of the running, and nodded to Steuber to go see to the door.

Steuber got to his feet, carefully set watch and book on the chair, and walked across the room — it was part-office, part-living room, part-library — to open the door. Baron reached one hundred and began at once to do sailor jumps. Steuber was talking in the doorway with one of the staff members from downstairs. Baron did ten sailor jumps and started running again, and Steuber left the room, closing the door behind him.

That was very unusual. Running, Baron frowned, trying to understand it. It must be important or Steuber would not have interrupted their routine this way. But if it were immediately dangerous Steuber would not have gone away without telling Baron about it. In any case, there was nothing to do but go on exercising.

It was a few minutes before Steuber came back, and when he did Baron was still running in place. Baron gasped, as he ran, "Almost done!" and Steuber hurried across the room to pick up the watch."

"One *hundred*!" cried Baron, coming down hard on his right leg. He stopped.

Steuber calculated, frowning massively at the watch. The watch looked small in Steuber's heavy gray hand. Finally, he said, "One minute, twelve seconds ahead."

"Good. What was that?"

"Man you better see," Steuber said. "You can tell better than me if he's telling the truth."

Baron said, "Oh?" He walked across the room, stripping off his T-shirt. "What does he say?"

"Says some people are going to rob this place."

Baron stopped in the doorway. Beyond him was the gleaming tile of a bathroom. He looked back at Steuber. "What do you think?"

"I can't tell those types. Maybe it's the truth, maybe not."

"Where is he?"

"Dining room."

"All right." Baron nodded and went into the bathroom and shut the door. He stripped off the bathing trucks, took a fast shower, and went out the other door wrapped in a white terrycloth towel. Steuber had laid fresh clothing out on the bed. Baron dressed, lit a cigarette, studied himself in the mirror. He was pleased. He went out to the other room and Steuber opened the farther door for him.

On the way down the stairs Baron said, "What is this man's name?"

"Heenan, he says."

"Heenan." Baron smiled and shook his head. "I dislike the Irish," he said. "A sloppy dirty people. My only prejudice."

He pushed open the door and went into the casino. It was barely three in the afternoon, so the casino was nearly empty.

The few customers looked up with surprise when Baron walked apparently out of the wall, because the door was invisible on the casino side. Steuber's bright idea, done as a surprise for Baron, his own little addition to the plans. Baron had tried to look pleased when Steuber first showed it to him, complete and invisible, but these occasional reminders of Steuber's thickheadedness were something of a trial. It had never occured to him that the casino might be full of customers sometime when Baron wanted to go up or downstairs. When Baron, as gently as possible, pointed it out to him, Steuber was chagrined, going around looking hangdog till Baron told him it was all right, it was actually a good gimmick, giving the customers an extra taste of the spice of adventure they were really coming to Cockaigne in search of.

In the dining room the Irishman was tucked away in an inconspicuous corner with two stickmen from the casino flanking him at the table. At Baron's arrival and gesture they went away. Baron sat down across from the Irishman and Steuber sat at Baron's right.

Baron said, "What's this stupid story?"

The Irishman looked aggrieved. That's what the breed did best, looked shifty and aggrieved. "It's no stupid story," he said. He was heavy-set and very pale of skin, with very black hair. "It's the truth," he said.

"Some people are going to rob this island." Baron put contempt and scorn and total disbelief into his voice.

But now the Irishman looked truculent, the other expression his sort found habitual. "You don't want to believe me," he said, "the hell with you."

Steuber lightly slapped his face. "Don't talk like that," he said.

The Irishman put his hand to his face, where the white skin was turning red in a design like fingers. His eyes widened and he said, "I didn't come here for trouble, I don't want trouble."

Baron said, "How do you know these people are going to rob the island?"

"They wanted me to go in with them, run the boat."

"But of course you were too honest for such a thing."

"I would of done it," the Irishman said truculently. "Only I wasn't good enough for them."

"They changed their minds about you?" Baron could see how it was possible, given this man.

"Somebody tried to kill me," the Irishman said. "I went on home and somebody tried to kill me, and I don't go for that."

"So you want revenge."

"It ought to be worth something to you, knowing about it in advance."

Baron smiled. "You want money?"

"You don't need charity," the Irishman told him.

Steuber raised his heavy hand and held it where the Irishman could see it. "You watch your mouth," he said.

Baron said, "It's all right, he doesn't know any better. Who are these people who plan to rob me?"

"There's a guy named Parker, and one named Grofield, and one named Salsa. They'll get somebody else to run the boat, I don't know who."

"It's just four of them?"

"That all that's doing the job. They got some kind of syndicate money behind them."

"Karns?" Baron raised his eyebrows. "Is that moron Karns behind this?"

It would make sense. Karns and the organization he represented were unhappy about Baron's existence independent of them. He was aware of that, had been for some time, but he had never considered — what did it call itself? The Outfit, yes — he had never considered the Outfit a serious threat.

And then there was more. The Irishman said, "They're supposed to take you back to shore with them, turn you over to the Feds. If they do, the cops'll leave them alone."

"What's this? Are you sure of that?"

"They told me so," the Irishman said.

"Mr. Heenan, I believe you."

"'Cause it's the truth."

"Of course. And your manner is so open and aboveboard."

"What?"

"Never mind. When is this robbery to take place?

"I don't know exactly. Some time soon."

Baron got to his feet. "Very well. I am grateful, Mr. Heenan, and once this robbery has come to pass, you can be sure I will express my gratitude in cash. In the meantime, I'll be happy to have you as my houseguest."

"Not me," said the Irishman, getting abruptly to his feet. "I want to be off this island when they get here."

"No." Baron said to Steuber, "Find Mr. Heenan a quiet room in the other building."

"You can't do this," said the Irishman.

3

The island glowed like a stage-set in the Hollywood Bowl, surrounded by the darkness of the sea. Grofield sat in the boat slowly turning toward the piers, and as he stared at the island the background music around his head was harsh, strident, violent. This was the eighth day. Tonight it was going to happen.

Salsa was seated to his right, silent, calm, imperturbable, smoking a little cigar. They were both in black suits and ties, the suits tailored not to show the guns stowed beneath them.

It was a Saturday night, with the island at its most crowded. Boats choked the approach to the piers, bobbing at anchor, many containing private parties, spreading out over the black sea yellow lights and the sounds of laughter. People called from boat to boat, waving, laughing, not fully able to understand one another. Dinghies pulled in toward shore or back toward the boats, dark-suited men at the oars and bright-eyed bright-gowned women sitting facing them. Many of them laughed and waved at Grofield and the others in the new boatload threading through the earlier arrivals toward the pier.

Ashore, groups and couples clustered throughout the rock garden or strolled out onto the piers arm in arm. A dance band had been set up — Friday and Saturday nights only — in a cleared space on the right side of the main building, with a grassy open area under the sky for a dance floor. The waltz music, very schmaltzy, floated out over everything else, uniting all the sights and sounds, combining them into a cohesive whole. Beneath the music the people moved, on the boats and on the piers, amid the rock garden, slowly in the dancing space, in and out of the doors of the main casino, and to and from the cockpit at the back. Above, the sky was black, dead black, pinholed with stars. It was the night of the new moon, and the

102

sky looked wrong, out of kilter, with no moon in it.

Grofield said, "The last days of Pompeii."

Salsa turned his head. "What was that?"

"Nothing. I expect the ground to open up, flames come shooting out."

What he didn't expect was for Salsa to understand him. But Salsa grinned and said, "It reminds me very much of places the ladies used to take me."

It always surprised Grofield that Salsa was unembarrassed about having been once a gigolo. Grofield couldn't imagine what that must be like; some time, he'd like to talk to Salsa about it.

The boat bumped against the pier, bumped again, and stopped. Grofield and Salsa joined the others going up the steps. They moved slowly through the people, along the path toward the casino. Along the way they picked up their usual tails.

There were four of them, and Grofield had named them. The meek-looking one in the blue-gray suit and the steel-rimmed spectacles was Walter Mitty. The short one with the crewcut and the military bearing and the severe expression with Giggles. The lanky red-haired one with the freckles, his tie askew, was Casey, Crime Photographer. And the stocky balding one in the brown suit was Friar Tuck.

They were on the island every night, already in place when Grofield and Salsa got there. Grofield knew they were Feds because at one time or another they'd all been on his tail ashore. Usually, Walter Mitty and Giggles followed Salsa around the island while Casey and Friar Tuck hung around Grofield, but now and again they switched it around, probably to relieve the boredom.

Tonight they stuck to the regular dispersement. When Salsa went off around the casino toward the cockpit — Salsa really dug cockfighting and Grofield couldn't figure out why — Walter Mitty and Giggles went right along with him. Grofield, followed by Casey and Friar Tuck, went into the main building and stopped first in the dining room. One thing he could say

103

about this place, they had good food.

After dinner — Casey and Friar Tuck at a table between him and the door — he spent a while, as usual, in the casino, dropping most of his losings at the roulette table but giving some of the other games a play as well. Around nine-thirty Baron came out of his secret door and went over to talk to the cashier about something and then went back through his secret door again, and both times he created the stir among the newcomer customers these entrances and exits always inspired. Grofield had been baffled by the door at first — what kind of secret was that? — but finally decided it was just a public relations gimmick. Too bad Baron didn't look more like George Raft and less like Sly Sam the Used Car Man.

At ten o'clock Grofield went into the men's room, turned around, and was going back out just as Casey was coming in. They bumped into one another, accidentally, and Grofield's elbow pumped, his rigid hand drove fingers-first twice into the pit of Casey's stomach. In the press around the door, men constantly on the move in both directions, the action couldn't be seen. Grofield moved on as behind him Casey doubled over and began to retch.

He had a minimum of two minutes before Casey would have his wind, his balance, and his stomach back. He moved fast now, going by Friar Tuck, who was waiting in the main hallway outside, just as he had every other time in the past. Grofield gave Friar Tuck a guilty sidelong glance as he hurried by, and then gave him a second one because Friar Tuck hadn't noticed the first. But he got the second, looked around, didn't see Casey, and took off after Grofield, who was leaving the building.

Grofield went around toward the cockpit at almost a run, brushing by the other people on the path. When he got to the cockpit he kept going, and around behind it there was less light and no people. Grofield stopped, leaning in the semi-darkness against the building, and waited.

Friar Tuck came hurrying around the curve, breathing hard, and walked straight into a pistol butt between the eyes. He made a small sound in his throat and fell over sideways off the path.

Grofield put the pistol away again, dragged Friar Tuck farther from the light, and hurried back to do a better job on Casey.

He found Casey out in front of the main building, looking pale and staring this way and that. Grofield hurried up to him, his hand in the side pocket of his coat, and leaned close enough to say, "If I killed you you wouldn't like it. Let's go for a walk with no static."

Casey said, "What's the point? What do you get out of it? We won't bother you, so what the hell?"

"I hate people who read over my shoulder. Let's just move forward. Toward the dormitory, pal."

Casey went, reluctantly, and all the way he kept trying to explain to Grofield that Grofield didn't have to do any of this. Grofield took him around into the darkness beside the dormitory and hit him with the pistol butt and Casey lay down on the ground and stopped explaining things.

He looked at his watch: five after ten. Parker and Ross would be on their way in, would be landing in five minutes. Plenty of time.

Grofield moved on around behind the dormitory heading for the boathouses. Now he'd take out anybody on guard there, so Parker and Ross could land unseen.

But he went around the back of the building and there were two guys there with T-shirts on their backs and automatics in their hands, and one of them said, "That's far enough, Grofield. Now you come with us."

Grofield recognized them, and knew they were not Feds, they were Baron's men. And they knew his name. They talked and acted as though they knew everything. They talked and acted as though the operation was suddenly as sour as a brand new lemon.

The one that talked said, "Put your hands on top of your head Grofield, while we frisk you. Then we all go talk to Mr. Baron."

Grofield took his pistol out and started shooting. So did they.

He emptied the pistol into them, felt the stinging here and there on his body, threw the empty pistol at their heads as they went down, and went running off into the jungle.

4

Baron paced back and forth, back and forth. He was smoking, the cigarette stuck into a long black holder with innards guaranteed to remove all harmful elements from the smoke. Cigarettes tasted bland, lousy, awful, smoked through this holder, and usually he managed to forget to use it, but tonight he felt danger around his head, and feeling danger around his head made him remember to use the health-protecting holder.

Steuber was in the room with him, sitting stolid and patient in his regular chair. Heenan was there, too, and complaining about it. "I don't want them to see me," he kept saying, "I got troubles enough with those guys."

"You will have no more trouble with them after tonight," Baron told him. "No one will." But he was distracted even while he was saying it.

It had to be tonight. Every night since Heenan had pointed the two of them out, the ones called Grofield and Salsa, the anticipation and alarm and apprehension had been building in Baron, until now it was almost a relief to know it was over, that tonight had to be the night.

He'd been sure of it at quarter to ten, when the word was passed to him that the man called Salsa was in the process of getting rid of the two policemen who had been following him around the island every night. "Let him do it," Baron had said, the nerves tingling in his stomach. "Let him do it to both of them, and then watch him to see what he plans next. Stop him from doing any harm to anyone or anything else, just wait till you see what he intends to do, and then disarm him and bring him up here to me. And keep watching the other one, Grofield."

That was at quarter to ten. By ten of ten Salsa had divested himself of his police followers, and a minute later he had disappeared. Everyone was apologies, excuses, bafflement. "We don't know how he could have done it! Into a shadow, and through it, and gone!"

"Find him!" Baron screamed. "He's on the island, find him, find him, find him!" And took out his long black cigarette holder with fingers that trembled.

Heenan began to whine, and Baron told him to shut up, but it took Steuber's hand to convince Heenan to be quiet. Then Heenan sat and sulked, like a stubborn child forced to sit in a corner.

At two minutes to ten Salsa was found, on the dancing field, moving in the arms of an ugly fat fifty-year-old matron to the strains of a Viennese waltz. Two staff members fidgeted at the edge of the field till the waltz was finished, then collared Salsa and brought him upstairs.

Salsa's eyes went first to Heenan. "Now," he said. "Now I understand. You work for everybody, Heenan."

"Don't believe a word he says," Heenan shouted, telling Baron there was something to learn about Heenan if Baron was interested.

Baron was not interested. Other matters concerned him. "Where have you been? What were you doing?"

"I have been dancing."

"Steuber. Quickly, quickly, we don't have much time."

Salsa said, "What time is it?"

"Ten o'clock."

"Then it no longer matters," Salsa said, and the phone rang. Baron picked it up, his hand shaking. "Yes? What is it?"

It was Rudi, downstairs, telling him Grofield had started, just as Salsa had started. "Watch him," Baron said. "Keep him in sight." He hung up and turned back to Salsa. "Where were you? What were you doing?"

"I set three fire bombs," Salsa told him. "They will go off in a very few minutes."

"Where? Where are they?"

"The exact locations are hard to describe. It might take half

108

an hour to give you the precise idea."

Baron said, "Steuber. Find out."

While the two who had brought Salsa up held him, Steuber and his hands began to ask the questions. Salsa closed his eyes at once, went limp, and said no more, no matter how strenuously Steuber asked him.

Five after ten. Eight minutes after; the phone rang. It was Rudi again, and he was excited, too excited to talk. But two things came through clearly; Grofield had killed Bud and Arnold and had disappeared, and the casino was on fire.

"Get it out," Baron said. "Find Grofield. Get the fire out, and find Grofield."

"But the people," Rudi kept saying. "But the people."

It took Baron a minute to understand what Rudi meant, but then he got it. The fire wasn't really bad, not yet, was only in a back corner of the casino, but the casino had been full of people, all of whom were panicking, milling about, trying to get out of the building all at once, making it impossible for Rudi and the other staff men to get through and do something about the fire.

Then Rudi said, "The cockpit! The cockpit, too! Fire, on fire!"

Baron threw the phone across the room. "The third one," he said. He spun around and grabbed Heenan by the shirt-front and dragged him to his feet. "The third one!" he shouted. "Parker! Where is this bastard Parker?"

"I don't know, I don't know, how should I know?"

Baron threw him away as he'd thrown the phone and ran across the room to where Salsa still hung limp in the arms of the two staff men, with Steuber waiting patiently to one side.

Baron grabbed Salsa by the hair, held his head up. "Where's Parker?" he shouted. "Where's your other man?"

Salsa didn't open his eyes, but he smiled.

Baron raged around the room, furious with doubt and fear. There was an onyx desk set on his desk and he yanked it up, spilling out the pens, He rushed back to Salsa and slashed at his head with the desk set, hitting him till blood streamed down over Salsa's face and the staff men finally dropped him and stepped back, looking whitefaced and confused.

"Guns!" shouted Baron. "Guns, guns, where are the guns?"

It was minutes after ten. Steuber moved stolidly across the room, pulling his keys from his pocket, on his way to unlock the guns.

5

For the first time in his life, there was no background music.

Grofield sat against a treetrunk in pitch darkness, examining himself as best he could with half-numb fingers. So far as he could tell, he had been shot four times, but none of them serious; he didn't seem to be carrying any of the bullets with him. One had sliced through the fleshy inner part of his upper arm, a few inches above the elbow, leaving a strong ache like a Charley horse in its wake. Another had drawn a line across the top of his left shoulder, barely breaking the skin and leaving behind it a faint stinging feeling. The third had gone in his right side at the waist, through the spare tire he kept meaning to exercise off, and out again, with a burning sensation where it had gone in and a dull ache where it had come out. And the fourth had gone through the fatty part of his left leg, a couple of inches below the groin, causing more bleeding than all the other three wounds combined, but with practically no pain at all.

These were the first four times in his life he'd been shot. The experience took some getting used to.

But slowly he was getting his equilibrium back. He touched himself all over, stretching his arms and legs and found that everything was working all right, and then grinned in the darkness. "If that's the best they can do," he whispered, "then, what the hell."

The background music started again as he climbed up the tree to a standing position. Somber music, portentous. Would he get through? Would he get to the cavalry in time to save the settlers from the Indians?

His left arm was stiff and his left leg was slightly numb, but he could still navigate. He moved through the tangled growth back the way he had come, and for the first time he noticed the new flickering quality of the light ahead of himself.

The place was on fire! Salsa had done his part, the fires were started.

What the hell time was it? If Parker and Ross tried to land, and Baron's men were in control at the boathouses. . . .

Grofield hurried the rest of the way back to where he'd left the two guys who'd shot him — they'd come out worse than him, they were still lying there on their faces — and went past them toward the boathouses; up ahead of him he could hear the sounds of gunshots.

No good. He didn't have a weapon on him.

He went back to the two guys he'd killed, and found their guns, both Colt automatics. There were three rounds left in the clip of one of them, and five in the other. Carrying them both, Grofield headed toward the boathouses again.

A cabin boat was in toward shore, bobbing in the waves as though there were neither a man at the controls nor an anchor out. Three guys on shore, protected behind the wall of the boathouses, were firing at it, and occasionally there was a flash of a gunshot from the boat.

Grofield picked his spot, steadied his right hand with his left, and picked them off one two three, doing it so fast the third one didn't even have time to turn all the way around. Then he hurried on down to the water's edge and called, "Parker! Come on in!"

The boat limped in to shore, bumping against the dock beside the boathouses. Grofield came out on the dock and Parker tossed him a line and Grofield made the line fast.

Parked climbed out of the boat, tossing two light plastic suitcases ahead of him, and said, "What's gone wrong?"

Grofield waved his hands, with the guns in them. "They know about it, don't ask me how. I got rid of the Feds on my back, and then two of Baron's men put the arm on me. They knew my name, they acted as though they knew everything. I shot my way out of it, but I got hit a few times." He was proud of the offhand way he had said that, and at the same time knew

112

that with Parker there was no other way he could have said it. In fact, it would have been better to say nothing at all, but that cool he couldn't be.

Parker looked away toward the casino. "The place is burning. Salsa's working."

"What time is it?"

Parker checked his watch. "Twenty after."

"He should be down here by now with the first load."

That was the way it was supposed to work. Salsa would fire the main buildings, then in the confusion break into the cashier's cage in the casino, grab as much cash as he could carry, and come down to meet the rest at the boat. Then all of them but Ross would go back to finish cleaning the place out. By twenty after Salsa should already be here.

Parker said, "We better go look for him."

Grofield was looking toward the boat. "Where's Ross?"

"Dead." Parker nodded toward the three Grofield had taken care of. "They opened up too early, before we docked. They got Ross right away, because he was up at the wheel."

"It's a lemon, Parker, a big fat lemon."

"Let's go look."

They each picked up one of the plastic suitcases, empty now and ready to carry money. Grofield replaced his guns with two more fully loaded ones from the beach defenders, and then he and Parker walked up the path toward the main building.

Now it did look like the last days of Pompeii. The main building and the dormitory and the cockpit were all ablaze. Men and women were running around in circles, shouting and screaming; there was a crush of them down on the piers, trying to get off the island. Just beyond the piers, two yachts, trying to get away, had rammed into one another and stuck together, and now wallowed in a death-grip, both of them burning. Firelight bloodied the dark water around the island and the boats, picking out the bobbing heads of people swimming. An overturned dinghy floated like a comic afterthought, with several people in the water clinging to it.

113

Because it had so few windows, the casino was burning less furiously than the other two buildings. The cockpit was one yellow-red flame, and the dormitory looked unreal: a hollow black hulk with flames shooting from every window.

No one paid any attention to Grofield and Parker. A musician ran by, wild-eyed, his violin tucked up under his arm like a precious message. A guy Grofield recognized as the stickman from the roulette table rushed past in the opposite direction, still toting his rake.

Behind the main building the flames had leaped from the cockpit to the jungle itself. Crackling louder, the fire swept up the hill toward the two storage sheds, engulfing them, and then on toward the power plant.

Parker went into the casino first, and Grofield followed him. The main hallway was not yet burning, but flames were gobbling up the innards of the dining room, tables and chairs and draperies and carpeting and all; the dining room doorway glared like the gateway to Hell. To the right, fire flickered uncertainly in the casino. With no windows, brick and plaster walls, widely spaced furniture, the flames had trouble in here making headway.

Still, the casino was deserted, and the gate in the cashier's cage gaped open. Parker and Grofield hurried in there and Parker began to yank open drawers. "It's here," he said.

There were a few bills scattered on the floor, and the main drawers were not entirely full, so at least one other person had done a little looting on the way out. But he'd left more than he'd taken, so it was all right. Parker and Grofield opened their suitcases on the counter and began transferring the money.

The lights flickered, and then flickered again. Parker took a flashlight from his pocket, and the lights went out for good. Parker switched the light on, and they went on filling the suitcases. Between the flashlight and the firelight they could see well enough.

When the hidden panel in the far wall opened and the bulky guy came running into the room, came catapulting in as though he'd just raced down a long steep hill, Grofield looked up and at first saw that the form looked familiar and second realized who it was. Softly, he said, "Parker," and when he felt Parker look over, he nodded toward the guy, now coming to a stop in the middle of the room, looking around crazily, a gun waving in his right fist.

Parker looked, and called, "Heenan!"

Heenan hadn't seen them till then. Now he did see them, and recognized them. "It wasn't me!" he shouted, and started pulling the trigger, bullets spraying into the wall high above Grofield's head.

Grofield rested his right elbow on the suitcase and emptied a borrowed gun into the leaping silhouette in front of the flames. Besides him, he could see Parker doing the same. Between them they must have fired ten times.

In the sudden silence after all the shooting, Parker said, "I say we find Salsa upstairs."

They had all the cash from down here anyway. Grofield shut the suitcases, leaving the full one on the floor and carrying the other one. Ahead of him, Parker stooped and took the automatic from Heenan's fist, and then the two of them went through the open panel and up the stairs to the lightless second floor.

6

Baron crouched in the darkness under his desk, in the kneehole, waiting for whatever would happen next. He knew now that this stage of his life was done, no matter what. The gambling island of Cockaigne was destroyed. Even if he should manage to rebuild, from where would the customers come, now that this debacle had occurred? Beyond that, the Russians and the Cubans, as single-minded and dull-witted as the majority of men everywhere, unable to think about anything but their own petty global concerns, would be convinced, unshakably convinced, that this holocaust was the work of American counterespionage, that his "cover" (their word) had been broken, and that he was no longer of any use to them.

So Cockaigne was finished. But was Baron?

It was bad now. The men named Grofield and Parker were surely together on the island somewhere, and wouldn't they be seeking their comrade? Salsa lay inert on the floor a little way away, near the dead Steuber, whom Heenan had shot. . . .

That had been stupidity, stupidity compounded. Steuber had unlocked the cabinet where the handguns were kept, had swung wide the door, and suddenly Heenan was there, raging, terrified, clawing past Steuber, his hand closing on a Luger, an old gun, one from an earlier life. Steuber, rather than keep hold of the Irishman and wrest the gun away from him, had flung the stocky man away, with a grunt of impatience. The Irishman had landed heavily, and rolled, and had come up apoplectic. He was still close to Steuber, and Steuber took a step that brought him even closer, and he fired twice and Steuber fell over on his back.

That moronic Irishman. He had swiveled then, seeking out Baron, and had found him just as the lights flickered and went out. But he fired anyway, just once, as Baron leaped sideways in the sudden dark, and perhaps the sound of Baron hitting the floor had deceived him. In any case, he had done no more shooting, but had groped his way toward the stairs, Baron clearly hearing his progression across the room.

Baron himself was all turned around, and didn't dare move to find a familiar piece of furniture and orient himself, not till the Irishman's blundering footsteps had clattered away down the stairs. Then he had moved, and had just crawled into the side of the desk when he heard the firing begin downstairs.

He would not have heard any firing if the soundproofed door were shut, so Heenan must have left it open. Heenan himself necessarily was part of the gunplay down there, and the only ones Baron could think of who would be shooting at Heenan were Grofield and Parker, so those two were surely down there and would surely be coming up here. Baron crawled at once to the kneehole under the desk, crouched there in a ball, and waited to see what would happen.

He didn't have long to wait. An uncertain light edged nervously along the walls, telling him someone was coming up with a flashlight. The he heard their footfalls on the carpet in the room, and the beam of the light sprayed around once, and one of them said, "Here's Salsa."

"How is he?"

They all waited, Baron too, until the other voice said, "Dead. They beat his head in."

Baron frowned. Had he done that? He'd let himself get too overwrought, too hysterical.

Above him, around him, they were prowling through the room, the flashlight stabbing this way and that. The sessions of his life had made him a man who did not easily get attached to a place, a landscape or a room or a piece of furniture, but the time spent on Cockaigne and specifically in this room had been among the most pleasant days of his life and so he had not been able to avoid developing a certain sense of proprietorship, a sense that now was violated by these strangers come to rob him of his money, his business, his safe harbor, and perhaps even his

117

life. They prowled the room, hulking figures in the darkness behind their light's stabbing beam, and from his crevice in the furnishings Baron watched them with eyes that hated and feared.

For a few moments the legs of one of them were thick prison bars just inches from his face; over his head the interloper was poking about the desk, riffling the papers and going through the drawers. He found the cashbox in the bottom righthand drawer, and said with muffled eagerness, "Parker!" But he did not find Baron.

The cashbox didn't satisfy them. They went through the filing cabinet, hurling papers about in their haste, and ultimately they found the wallsafe behind Shakespeare in the bookcase.

These were crude men, unskilled brutes. They hacked at the safe and finally shot its face off, and pulled from its depths Baron's store of forged papers, his final private cash reserves, and the little flannel sacks of diamonds. Diamonds were sounder than any currency in the world, instantly convertible to cash in any civilized nation, readily transported and easily hidden. And, as he now watched, swiftly stolen.

They had brought a suitcase with them, and now it bulged with cash and diamonds. They closed it, and one of them said, "We'd better get out fast. The fire's worse down there."

The other one said, "Where's Baron, I wonder?"

"What do we care?"

Baron smiled a bitter smile, and the pale light receded, closed in at the far end of the room, confined itself in the stairwell.

Once they were gone, surely gone, Baron crawled out from beneath the desk. All was dark save the one window in this room, overlooking the front of the casino and the piers, and this window now showed a rectangle of dusky red. Baron hurried toward it, and looked out.

Was the whole island in flames? To his right the staff's sleeping quarters was a torch, a hollow shell sinking in on itself. To his left the jungle underbrush was burning, even down to the water's edge. And out in the water two yachts, crammed together in a letter Y, slowly circling like the center of a lazy whirlpool, burned like a campfire on the sea.

He pressed his forehead against the glass — the glass was warm, the carpet beneath his feet was warm, the wall against which he pressed his hand was very warm — and below him he could see the two figures emerge from the building, each carrying a suitcase, and hurry off through the flickering red in the direction of the boathouses.

Oh, would they! Baron turned, his eyes more accustomed to the darkness now, and found his way to the gun cabinet, still hanging open. He selected a Colt. 45, the United States Army model, checked to be sure the clip was full, and then made his way across the room and down the stairs to where the casino at last had grown hot enough for the flames to begin to make headway. He crossed his arms in front of his face and ran from the building, the hair on his forearms singeing with an audible sound and a disgusting smell.

Outside, the holocaust stunned him for a second. People, the fainted or the trampled, lay like unwanted rag dolls amid the rock gardens, sprawled on their faces. Others still ran this way and that, some calling out names, looking for the lost or looking to be found. More were milling about on the piers, from which the last boat had already left.

The whole island was a torch, lighting the sea around itself. The power plant at the peak of the island burned with a particular brilliance, the bright flames releasing from the tonguelike tips great billows of black smoke, which were swept away westward on the prevailing winds, blending with the black sky, putting out the brilliant white dots of the stars.

Through the heat and the light Baron ran, cursing in four languages, the automatic hanging like a club from the end of his right arm. He hurried past the collapsing hulk of the staff's quarters, down the path to the boathouses, and saw the two of them ahead of him, striding toward the boat, the suitcases swinging at their sides. He closed the distance between them, and just as they reached the boat and tossed the suitcases aboard he stopped, and leveled his arm out straight, and twice he fired.

One of them fell on the dock, one into the boat. In the uncertain light, in his excited frame of mind, he had no idea whether the shots had been fatal or not, but he didn't care. A .45 automatic hits hard, no matter where it hits, hard enough at the very least to knock them out. The one on the dock was either dead now or would burn to death later. The one in the boat was either dead now or would drown later. In any case, there was no time to spare on them now.

He ran to the boat and climbed aboard it, and instantly realized this was the boat the boys had intercepted and sent on its way one noontime a couple of weeks ago. The boat had clearly not contained customers, the way it was behaving, so he had ordered some staffmen out to question its occupants, and after circling the island once it had gone away. So it had been a reconnaisance after all, a first trip by these idiots now dead and dying.

Baron knew boats. He got this one started right away, and headed straight out to sea. He fled half an hour on a line due south before moving away from the wheel and then the first thing he did was go back to the body on the deck.

It was not Grofield, not any face Baron had ever seen before. He had never seen Parker, so this must be he. He looked different from what Baron had anticipated. No matter; he was dead and finished. Baron threw the body overboard.

He set his course for Mexico.

7

Grofield lay in darkness, his mind uncertain, wavering between lucidity and delirium. He only kept control of one idea: if Baron found him he would die. He couldn't defend himself against Baron now, and Baron would surely want to kill him, so the answer was he would die. To keep it from happening, he must keep tight his grip on the springs.

In and out of consciousness, in and out of pain, Grofield kept his grip on the springs.

For the fith time tonight, for the fifth time in his life, Grofield had been shot. This one, he was afraid, this one was much worse than the other four. The pain was too diffuse, too changing and echoing, for him to be certain exactly where the bullet had entered him, but he believed it was in the back just below the left shoulder. He also believed the bullet was still in him, since he felt no equivalent pain at the top left side of his chest.

The hit had knocked him out for a while, he wasn't sure how long. He'd come to slowly, being first aware that he was in a vehicle of some kind, in something that moved and rocked, and then coming to understand that he was in a boat. Because he was lying on something soft, he'd assumed at first he was in a bed or bunk and that Parker was operating the boat. But then he came closer to the surface of the world and realized he was lying on something too lumpy and oddly shaped to be a bed, and when at last he opened his eyes he found himself staring into the dead eyes of Ross, an inch away.

That shocked him the rest of the way to consciousness. He was on deck, in against the side wall, lying atop dead Ross. And the man at the wheel was not Parker, definitely not Parker.

He remained conscious that time long enough to think and long enough to act. He knew he was no match for Baron now, and that meant he had to hide, and the only place to hide on board a boat was somewhere below.

It was possible to get below without passing Baron at the wheel. Grofield crawled, pulling himself along with his left arm dragging, and when he got to the ladder he crawled backward to it, doing most of the work with his legs, and he was still so weak he fell part of the way, landing hard on the carpet down below, knocking the wind out of himself, and some of the clarity, for a few minutes.

When he was aware of himself again, he lay on his back in the middle of the main cabin, looking around, trying to find a hiding place. But everything was so compact on a boat like this, so small and so open, no wasted space or hidden corners anywhere.

Compact. Wasn't there a fold-up bed concealed in one wall? There was, he knew there was. This boat was supposed to sleep eight, and that was accomplished with the help of a sofa that converted into a bed and another bed that folded conveniently away into the wall.

He had to fight great dizziness and weakness and a wandering mind, but he managed to rise, and to find the way to open the bed, and to lower it to the floor. But there was no excess space behind it, no place for him to hide.

His exertions were making the wound bleed more; the back of his coat and his sleeve were heavy and sopping and gluelike with blood. There were stains on the carpet, but that couldn't be helped.

And there was more to be done, if he wasn't to die here, as helpless as a kitten. He wrestled the mattress off the bed and onto the floor. Sometimes lying down, sometimes kneeling, he tugged and pushed and mangled the mattress through the doorway into the forward cabin and, folded lengthwise in half, under one of the beds there. Baron, when he looked, could simply believe the owners had for some reason of their own brought an extra mattress aboard, unless Baron was familiar with this sort of boat, and knew about hideaway beds, in which case all this struggle was for nothing, and he would die cowering in a hole in the wall behind a bed, like a silent movie lover discovered by an irate cross-eyed husband. In any case, Baron would be looking for him, that much was certain.

But there was nothing a man could do other than his best. Grofield made his way back to the center cabin, up onto the twanging springs of the bed, and finally half-erect in the rectangular hole behind it, looking like a three-dimensional painting of despair.

He got the bed up, with great difficulty, and then he crouched in darkness, leaning against the walls at this back and right side, his fingers clutching the springs. He must now let the bed fall open. He must not lose consciousness so much that he should lose his balance and let the bed and himself crash down and out into plain sight.

He knew Baron would go back within the hour to throw the two bodies overboard, and he knew immediately afterward Baron would begin the search. He could only hope Baron would not find him here and would believe Grofield had gone overboard.

But time passed, and there was no sound of Baron searching. Being in and out of awareness so much, it was hard for Grofield to tell how much time had passed, and so he kept believing it had been less than an hour, it must have been less than an hour or Baron would have begun his search by now.

He believed this as five hours went by, then hours. The bleeding had stopped, the blood had caked and dried over the wound. For a while he shook with chills, a terrible cold he feared was the cold of death, and then for another while he ran with sweat and his face was fiery hot with fever. And still, in his lucid moments, he believed that less than an hour had transpired since he had closed himself away in this vertical coffin.

After fifteen hours he gave up. His stiff fingers loosened on the bed springs, his tense body relaxed, and he crashed forward, the bed opening and landing hard on its retractable legs, Grofield bouncing on the springs and then lying there sprawled out with his face against the springs.

Midday sunlight poured through the windows, shining on him. He was exposed, vulnerable, open to his enemy, but he was no longer aware of it. He had passed out again.

8

At noon on Sunday Baron came to land, not because he had gone as far as he wanted but because the boat ran out of fuel. He had been fleeing south for nearly fourteen hours, and the scrubby rocky beach off to his right was Mexico, about two hundred miles south of the border, about twenty miles south of the village of Pesca.

He beached the boat, then went below in search of food. He hadn't eaten since last night, hadn't slept since the night before.

He noticed nothing wrong in the main cabin. Fatigue was part of the explanation, plus relief at having escaped once again, plus impatience to be off and moving.

There was little to eat on board. A box of Ritz crackers, some liquor and soft drinks, some cheese spread and a few cans of soup. Baron made himself a quick meal, tomato soup and crackers and cheese and some bourbon straight from the bottle, and then he went back on deck for a look around.

The area was deserted, as far as the eye could see. The land sloped upward gradually from the sea, then levelled out toward the distant horizon, and everywhere Baron could see it was the same; tan dry grassless earth, littered with small rocks and pocked with hardy clumps of desert greenery. The shallow water all around the boat was scattered with boulders.

This was some of the wildest country Baron had ever seen. Gazing at it from the deck of the boat, he was filled with misgivings. If only the fuel had lasted a hundred miles longer, enough to get him to Tampico, to civilization.

All right, that wasn't important. He was free of the island, that was enough. Now there was nothing for it but to cross this semidesert until he found a road, a town, any sign of human habitation. From there on everything would be all right, everything would be fine.

He gathered up the suitcases, full of his worldly possessions, and went over the side. He waded to shore, holding the suitcases high because he didn't know if they were waterproof or not, and when he reached dry land he set the suitcases down and sat awhile on a boulder to collect his breath and his thoughts.

He felt naked, without Steuber at his side. Steuber had been with him for a quarter of a century; it seemed impossible that Steuber now was dead. As though he and Steuber had somehow become Siamese twins, and it wasn't possible for the one to be alive without the other one still living.

But that was nonsense. Self-interest, that was paramount. Steuber had merely been an adjunct, a crutch, an assistance in the problem of self-preservation. The problem still remained, without Steuber, and he could still face and solve it, without Steuber.

He got to his feet, picked up the suitcases, and started walking.

He walked west, due west, toward the sun. The suitcases, which had at first seemed so light, quickly became heavy, forcing him to make frequent stops for rest. He had brought the bourbon bottle along and used it sparingly to rinse out his mouth when it became too dry, but he soon saw he wouldn't be able to survive too long without water.

There had to be a road, somewhere. He didn't know Mexico very well, but he was under the impression there were plenty of north-south roads, coming down from the border toward Mexico City. He was surprised there wasn't one skirting the shore, a scenic route for tourists who liked to look at the ocean.

Walking was not too easy. From time to time he stumbled on the stones — the ground was littered everywhere with stones — and then the suitcases banged painfully against his shins. The sun was very hot, the air was humid and heavy. Baron soon took off his coat and rolled up his shirt sleeves, but within fifteen minutes his clothing was drenched with sweat.

Still, he wasn't worried. This wasn't the Sahara desert, it was

Mexico, and Mexico was a civilzed country. There would be a road, sooner or later, and he would walk until he reached it.

His shoes constricted his feet; within them his feet were burning. His arms ached from the weight of the suitcases. He blinked perspiration constantly out of his eyes, and when he licked his lips he tasted salt. More and more frequently he found it necessary to stop and rest.

He evolved a procedure, a method. He moved by the numbers, trudging forward two hundred paces and then stopping, setting the suitcases down, sitting on one of the cases or on the ground while he counted ten inhales and ten exhales, and then getting up and moving forward again another two hundred paces. In his imagination he could hear Steuber just behind him, counting aloud as he had always counted for the exercises. It was almost as though, if he were to turn suddenly, he would see Steuber there, stolid and patient, his watch held in the palm of his left hand.

The exercises had not been wasted. If he were not in perfect physical condition now, a man of his age, walking across this barren land this way, it might kill him. At the best it would take an impossible amount of time, maybe even result in his having to spend a night in the open air, lying on the rock-strewn ground.

The sun inched down the sky ahead of him, slowly becoming a nuisance, burning into his eyes, making him squint, making it difficult for him to see, so he tripped more often. He was most of the time out of breath, but he kept doggedly to the same pace, two hundred steps and a ten-breath rest, two hundred steps and a ten-breath rest.

He trudged slowly across the afternoon, the suitcases hanging from his arms like blocky weights hung there for a punishment. Dust puffed up around his feet at every step, and when his shoe brushed the stones they clicked together like pool balls. The landscape was unchanging, unpopulated.

In late afternoon the oppressive humid heat began to ease just a little, and the sun shrank from a white hell in the the middle of the sky to a more comfortable yellow-red ball falling slowly toward the horizon. Still, even yellow-red it was too bright to look at directly, and Baron still had to shuffle forward squinting, his face covered with dust, his clothing heavy with the dust intermixed with perspiration. From time to time he had sipped at the bourbon bottle to cut the layers of dust in his mouth, but he hadn't thought to bring any of the crackers or the other food from the boat, so now he felt a little lightheaded. But that was good, it made it easier to keep moving.

By sunset he had walked a full twenty-one miles due west from the sea and had not yet come to a road. As the sun edged down out of sight far away in front of him, as the swift evening closed toward night, Baron began at last to feel real apprehension. Where had he landed, on what mistaken, lost, useless, forgotten shore had he cast himself?

It took a conscious effort of will to keep from running.

When he saw the man, he at first didn't recognize him for what he was, but mistook the seated figure in the failing light for only one more of the occasional boulders he passed. It was ahead of him, and as he came closer it seemed to him the boulder was odd somehow, wrong somehow. And then he recognized it for a man, squatting on a low rock, his rounded back toward Baron.

Baron came forward, stumbling on the stones, forgetting his count. His suitcases banged the sides of his legs, hitting the raw places where they'd been hitting all afternoon, but he hardly noticed.

In a way, he was astonished. In a way, he hadn't actually expected ever to see another human being again.

He was so excited he made the mistake first of speaking English: "Hello! Where am I, where the hell's a road?"

The other man was just as startled as Baron. He leaped to his feet, half-stumbled as he backed away. He was an old man in gray and white clothing, clean but very ragged. He had the deeply lined face of an Indian, and his eyes showed the whites in his surprise and fear.

Baron realized the mistake with the English and leaped to another tongue. "*Wo ist die autobahn? Habern sie—*"

No, no, that was wrong too, that was German. In his confusion and haste, backing away from English he had switched automatically to his native tongue.

Spanish, that was what he wanted, Spanish, but for just a second there was none of it in his head. He floundered, then the Spanish word for road came to him — *camino* — and the rest of the language followed.

So now he said, in Spanish, "I beg your pardon, I did not mean to startle you. I have been walking, looking for the road."

"Road? You want the road?" The old man spoke a dialect full of clicks and gutturals, so Baron could barely understand him.

Baron nodded. "Yes. I want to continue my journey."

The old man waved his hand. "This is the road," he said.

Baron looked. There was almost no light left, but now he could make out the ruts, the hump in the middle, the swath across this land cleared of stones and pebbles. This was the road, he was standing on the road, the old man had been sitting beside the road.

He said, "Where does this road go?"

The old man pointed south. "Aldama," he said. He pointed north. "Soto la Marina."

Neither name meant anything to Baron. He said, "Which way leads to a bigger road, with automobiles and trucks?"

The old man pointed north again, toward Soto la Marina. "At the village," he said, "you must take the road west. To Casa. To Petaqueno. To Ciudad Victoria, which is a great city."

Ciudad Victoria. That was the first name Baron knew. He said, "How far is that, Ciudad Victoria?"

"From the village, perhaps more than one hundred kilometers."

One hundred kilometers. Sixty miles, a little more. Baron said, "No cars before there?"

"Sometimes at Casas. Or Petaqueno, very often."

"And how far to your village, to Soto la Marina?"

The old man shrugged. "Five kilometers."

Three miles. "Is there somewhere I could sleep there tonight?" Because another three miles was the most Baron would walk without sleep and food and water.

The old man said, "In my house, near the village. I am going home now, come with me."

"Good."

They started walking along the dimly seen track, and the old man said, "The suitcases are heavy?"

"No. Not too heavy."

"They have valuable things inside them?"

Baron turned to look at him. Was this old fool thinking of robbing him? But he was too old, too frail, there couldn't be anything to fear from him. Baron said, "Just some clothing and things like that. Nothing valuable."

"Perhaps an electric razor," said the old man.

"No."

The old man was a moron. He did plan to rob Baron tonight, while Baron slept, but he was too stupid to keep his mouth shut and so he'd given the game away.

The only thing to do was take care of the old man as soon as they got to his house, hut, hovel, whatever he lived in. Knock him out, tie him up, so Baron would be able to sleep unworriedly all night.

They walked the rest of the way in silence, each full of his own thoughts, and the last of the evening's light faded away, leaving a world so dark Baron had only the sound of the old man's sandals to keep him from straying off the road. He couldn't see a thing and couldn't understand how the old man could see. Although it probably wasn't seeing after all but simply knowing the road for all of his life.

Ahead of them, the smallest of lights flickered, an anemic yellow. The old man said, "My house."

As they got closer, Baron saw that the light was a candle inside a small dirt hut. The window through which the light gleamed was simply a square hole in the thick dirt wall, with

130

neither frame nor glass.

"A poor place," the old man said, apologizing.

"No matter," Baron said, and it was true. What did it matter where he slept tonight? Tomorrow night he would sleep in the Mexico City Hilton.

The door was made of various gray pieces of wood haphazardly nailed together, the final result hung from cloth hinges embedded in the wall on the left side. The old man pushed this door open cautiously, as though it had fallen apart more than once before, and motioned to Baron to precede him. "My house," he said again.

Baron went in.

The old man came after him, crowding him in the doorway, saying, "I wish you to meet my son."

The man rising from the wooden table in the middle of the room was not old, not frail, not small. He was huge, and he was smiling beneath his mustache.

Behind Baron, the old man was saying, "This gentleman has many valuable things in his suitcase. . . ."

Baron turned for the doorway, but it was too late.

9

Early morning sunlight tugged at Grofield's eyelids, urging him awake. Reluctantly, mistrustfully, he allowed his eyes to open, he allowed his mind to begin to question where he was.

The boat. He remembered.

What time was it? What day was it? Not yet midnight when he'd left the island, and he could vaguely remember sunlight as he'd lain on the open unmattressed bed, and he could remember even more vaguely crawling from that bed in darkness onto the far more comfortable carpeting of the floor, and now there was sunlight again, and he was still lying on the floor, and he couldn't begin to work out how much time had passed or what day it was supposed to be.

Or where Baron was. Where was Baron?

He moved, tentatively, and was pleased to find that nearly everything worked fine. Everything but the left arm. That didn't want to work at all. It felt like the Tin Woodman's left arm, in need of oiling.

He wondered about himself, how sick or healthy he was, how weak or strong. He kept testing, trying this and venturing that, and the first thing he knew he was on his feet. He felt shaky, a little dizzy, and hungrier than he could ever remember being, but he was on his feet.

He could even walk, if he was careful. Being careful, he moved around the open bed and over to the kitchen area of the cabin, and there he found some food and drink. He ate three cans of soup, cold and undiluted, spooning the stuff straight out of the can, mixing it with crackers and spoonfuls of cheese spread and long swallows of whiskey. He sat in the chair by the formica counter and ate everything in reach, and when he was done he felt as though he might survive.

He was feeling good enough now to begin to think, to try to

132

figure out what had happened. The boat was grounded, in close to shore. He was obviously the only one aboard her, so it figured Baron had gone ashore and taken off with the suitcases full of loot. What he couldn't figure was why Baron had never bothered to look for him, why he'd left this loose string untied behind him.

In any case, the situation was bad. He'd been unconscious at least one day and night, making it probably Monday and maybe Tuesday. The island had been demolished according to plan, but the plan had been demolished too. Parker and Salsa and Ross were all dead, Baron had the money and the diamonds, and Grofield was stuck God knew where with a bullet in his back.

He shook his head, thinking about how bad the situation was, and then he went slowly and carefully up on deck. The body of Ross was gone, too, he saw, and looked the other way, toward shore.

Bad. Desert type of place, nothing in sight.

Still, Baron must have known what he was doing, must have had some reason to stop here. Maybe just out of sight there was a city. Monterey. Or Corpus Christi. Or Eldorado.

A stray idea occurred to him. Was there any chance he might catch up with Baron, get the handle back? He didn't know how much of a lead Baron had on him, maybe a full day's worth, but was there nevertheless a chance it could be done?

The background music began, floating around his head. Arabic, partly, with threads of international intrigue. Foreign Legion, decidedly. A very Gary Cooper sort of role.

He felt his pockets and found a crumpled pack of cigarettes and some matches. It was good the cigarette he lit was rumpled and bent, it added a dash of Humphrey Bogart to the blend. The cigarette in the corner of his mouth, he leaned on the rail at the bow and gazed toward shore.

What the hell, he'd have to go that way in any case. He couldn't stay here. If he were to get the medical attention he needed, he had to find civilization, and that inevitably meant following in Baron's footsteps. If, in so doing, he caught up with Baron, so much the better.

He'd have to prepare. He had no idea how far a town or city might be, or how much trouble he'd have reaching it. What might be a simple walk for Baron, hale and healthy, could be rough for Grofield the way he was right now.

He went back down into the cabin, in search of food. He'd left a few crackers, and these he stuffed in his shirt pocket. An empty Jack Daniels bottle would serve to carry water, and a half-full Jack Daniels bottle would serve to carry Jack Daniels. A wedge of American cheese went into his trouser pocket.

In a closet in the fore cabin he found a yachting cap. A hat would be good protection from the sun; he put it on and went up on deck, carrying the two bottles with him.

On deck, he changed his mind about one detail and decided it was foolish to carry two bottles, it would just weigh him down. He took three or four swigs from the bottle with the whiskey in it, then tossed it overboard. Water would be more useful this time.

He clambered with difficulty over the side, waded through the shallow water, having trouble keeping his balance with all the rocks and stones underfoot, and made his first rest stop when he reached dry land.

The morning sun was still low on the horizon, making the sea gleam like a shield. To walk away from the sea, Grofield should head due west, and this meant keeping his back to the sun. Simple.

A halo of music. It was a martial air now, with a muted touch of wistfulness in it, a minor key. There'll always be an England, a France, some damn place. Grofield moved out in time to the music, walking on his shadow stretched out in front of him, a thin elongated El Greco silhouette of himself.

He was somewhat unsteady, both because of the wound and because of the whiskey. Still, he kept due west and he made fairly good time. The shadow of himself he walked on slowly shrank as the sun rose higher in the sky behind him, and when the shadow was no taller than the original he became aware of the heat.

It was building slowly but steadily. The early morning had been pleasant, if not cool, but now heat was massing on the floor of the world, stacked like woolly invisible blankets through which he had to walk. The sun beat on the back of his neck, and he knew for sure he already had a bad burn there. His left shoulder ached, but not badly.

He tried to make the water last, but he kept being thirsty, very thirsty. He hummed silently as he walked, and dreamed of other things, different times and places, the faces of people he knew and once had known.

He found he was walking *toward* the sun.

"No," he said aloud. He turned around, very carefully. The shadow was a dwarf now, bunched up before his feet on the rock-bedraggled ground. He walked again.

"This was very stupid," he whispered, and realized he was thirsty again, and held up the bottle to see it was empty. He grimaced at it, disappointed with the behaviour of the damn thing, and let it fall. It shattered on a rock.

He fell, not too badly, and got up again. He walked on, and fell again, and this time he didn't get up. "I'm sorry," he whispered into the ground, apologizing to himself. "I shouldn't have left the boat."

He had been asleep, or unconscious, he couldn't tell which, and then suddenly he was awake again. He rolled over on his back, unmindful of the stones, regardless of the sun's light, and stared into the sky, and he thought he saw Parker coming down out of the sky on a cloud.

"Sacrilege, Parker," he said aloud, and smiled, and closed his eyes.

FOUR

1

Parker said, "There's something there." He pointed down at the ground.

"I see it," said the pilot.

England said, "If that's our man, and he's alive, we have no legal right to take him off Mexican soil."

Parker had no time for England's worries. He was staring toward the ground, trying to see suitcases. The helicopter lowered, and he could see it was a man down there, but no suitcases. Then the man rolled over on his back, staring up at the helicopter with its bulging transparent front bubble, the three men in it staring down at him, and Parker saw it wasn't Baron. It was Grofield, and that was impossible.

Parker had last seen Grofield on the dock by the boathouses back at the island, just before he'd been shot. The bullet had hit him high on the right leg, spinning him around and throwing him to the ground, knocking him cold, but that was the second bullet. The first bullet had hit Grofield; Parker had seen him jerk forward.

When he'd come out of it, back there on the flaming island, the boat and the suitcases were gone, and a raging petulant England was standing over him, shaking him, shouting that Baron had gotten away. Parker had had no time nor inclination to look for Grofield's body. There had been so many there, he'd just assumed one of them had to belong to Grofield.

The important thing was the money, and it figured the money was with Baron. According to England, Baron was on the boat, headed south.

Parker couldn't stand then, though he kept trying. "Where?" he said. "Are you on him?"

"No. In all this wreckage you people caused, we lost him. We know he was heading south, it makes sense he'd try to get to

Mexico, Cuba's too far for him to reach, he must know that."

"Get on him," Parker said. "Find him." He was still trying to stand, still falling back. "And fix this leg," he said. "Fix it. Fix it. I can't stand on it, fix it."

They took him out to a Navy ship on a launch, where a guy in white cut off his trouser leg and somebody else in white, who said he was a doctor, probed around and took out the bullet. "You ought to stay off this," he said.

"I can't," Parker told him. England was still hanging around, yapping in his ear, wanting to know where he'd been the last week, why he'd ditched his tail, why Grofield and Salsa had suddenly turned on the men assigned to watch them at the island. Instead of getting on Baron, England stood around talking about ancient history.

When Parker told him to shut up and find Baron, England said, "We can't look now, it's the middle of the night, everywhere but on that damn island. It's still burning, do you know that?"

"When?" Parker asked him.

"When? Right now. Look at the red on the Porthole, that's *fire*, man."

"When do you look for Baron?"

"When it gets light. In the morning."

Parker said, "Nobody goes to him but me. They don't go to him without me, that's got to be part of it."

The doctor said, "Quit moving around. Do you want me to patch you up or don't you?"

England said, "Why? Why should we take you along. Your part is finished, Parker, don't you know that?"

Parker told him, "He isn't anywhere you can put a legal collar on him, not yet. That's where you want him, isn't it? Where you can put a legal collar on him. You still need me, to take him from where he is and put him where you can grab him."

England didn't like it. He chewed it like a cow chewing its cud, and finally he nodded and said, "We'll see," and Parker knew that was that. He told the doctor, "I'll sleep till morning if you'll get off me."

The doctor was irritated. He left without saying anything.

In the morning, other people did the searching. "We could do nothing by ourselves," England said. "We have a hundred men doing the searching."

Carey was back with England now, the two of them sitting with Parker on the deck of the Navy ship. Carey said, "All they'll do is find Baron, let us know where he is. Then we'll go get him."

Parker still had trouble standing, and almost as much trouble sitting. He was stretched out on his side on a cot set up on deck. He felt like a fool, and he felt impatient. He said, "Your hundred men better be good."

But they didn't find anything, not all day long, and after dark they had to quit again. Parker was up by now, limping up and down the metal corridors, raging. "You need a hundred men to zip your fly, you people. You and Karns' crowd, you're all alike. No one of you can do a damn thing, so you figure a whole crowd of you can do everything."

Carey had gone away, and only England was around to listen to it. "We'll find him," he kept saying. "He must have gone to shore by now, and tomorrow that's where the search will concentrate. Every possible inch of Gulf coastline he could have reached."

"They'll lose their planes by morning," Parker said.

But in the morning they found the boat, run aground on a barren stretch of Mexican coastline about two hundred miles down from the border. "They saw the boat," England told Parker, "but they didn't see Baron."

"The question is, did Baron see them?"

"They said the boat looked abandoned," England said. "It looked to them as though he'd run out of gas."

"Do we go look?"

"Surely." England nodded his head, showing he was sure. "They're getting a chopper ready for us now."

A chopper turned out to be a helicopter, a rickety-looking thing like a cross between a Sten gun and a beanie, with a plexiglass bubble in front where the pilot and passengers sat. Only three of them were going, Parker and England and the pilot. England didn't say anything to the pilot about who Parker was, and the pilot didn't ask.

141

The ship they'd been on had been moving south all night and lay now off the Mexican coast, about forty miles from where the boat had been sighted. Parker and England got there in the helicopter in less than half an hour. The pilot landed near the beach, and waited at his controls while Parker and England went over to the boat.

Parker could walk on the leg now, but stiffly; he was bruised on that side from hip to knee. A bullet from a Colt .45 punches more than it cuts, and the one that had hit Parker had left him with a leg that operated all right but that ached as though it had been worked over with a baseball bat.

Walking toward the boat, limping, he wished he was armed. England had a service revolver on him, but it was tucked away in its hip holster now under England's suitcoat. The boat looked empty, but that didn't mean anything.

The leg gave him trouble, wading the last part out to the boat. England had to help him aboard, and then they searched the boat and found it deserted but odd. The hideaway bed in the main cabin was standing open, without its mattress, which Parker found shoved under a bed in the fore cabin. He and England pulled it out of there gingerly, both of them half expecting to find a body rolled in it, but there was nothing. Just the mattress, no reason, no explanation.

There were bloodstains on the carpet in the main cabin, so maybe Baron had been hit, though Parker had no idea who might have shot him. There was also evidence that a couple of meals had been eaten down here, and the yachting cap Parker had put on that first day he'd seen the island, when he'd gone out in this boat with Yancy, that cap was now missing.

So were the suitcases. Man in a yachting cap, carrying two suitcases, probably wounded. "He'd head inland," Parker said, thinking of the suitcases. "Let's go in after him."

"We have no jurisdiction," England said.

"That's why you brought me along, remember?"

England said, "You think you can get him to the States from here? We might be better off asking the Mexican police to pick him up for us. They'll usually cooperate in a case like this."

Parker shook his head. "I hear Baron's got connections with Cuba. Mexico still recognizes Cuba, right? Baron contacts the Cuban embassy, Cuba says he's ours we want him, Mexico lets him go."

England said, "I never liked this operation, not from the beginning. If things had gone the way you wanted, you'd have doublecrossed us, you'd have taken the money, left Baron, and disappeared."

"You wanted us to help," Parker told him. "But you didn't ask right."

"Is that what it was?" England looked at him. "I don't understand you. Why should I trust you now?"

"Because you don't lose anything. Without me you don't get Baron at all. With me you get Baron maybe."

"I've got you now," England said. "If I let you go, then I don't have Baron and I don't have you either."

"You don't want me. Remember? You're a specialist."

England said, "So are you. I'm beginning to find out in what."

Parker could visualize the suitcases moving away across the horizon, while he and this fool stood here talking crap. England didn't know about the suitcases, because Parker had let him understand the loot had burned up in the fire back on the island. England had believed it because it satisfied his need for poetic justice. But now there was no justification for Parker being in such a hurry, and if he kept on pushing, England might begin to wonder.

Still, England himself should be in a hurry. Parker said to him, "Make up your mind. Do you want Baron or not?"

England shrugged. "All right," he said, "I'll see it out. I was told to cooperate, I'll cooperate. But if we ever get our hands on Baron through you I'll have a heart attack."

They went back to the helicopter and told the pilot what they wanted; their quarry would be heading west, or toward the nearest town, or both. "We don't know how long ago he left," England said, "so we aren't looking just for him. We're also looking for signs that he's passed a certain way, so we'll be sure which way he's headed."

For the next hour and a half they made tic-tac-toe in the sky, north and then south and then west, north and then south and then west, until ahead of them they saw the black man-shape spread out on the ground and Parker pointed forward, saying, "There's something there."

The helicopter lowered, and Parker saw no suitcases, and then he made out that the figure on the ground was Grofield, which was impossible.

The pilot landed twenty yards away, and Parker hurried across the rocky ground, limping, wanting to get there before England, to keep Grofield from saying anything he shouldn't.

Grofield had his eyes closed, and very faintly he was smiling. He looked as though he'd been wandering out here for a week, with dirt caked on his face, with his lips dry and cracked, his clothing filthy. Parker knelt beside him and said, low and fast, "England's with me. Keep mum on the money."

Grofield opened his eyes as England came running up. Grofield said, "Come off it, Parker, you're a mirage."

Parker said, "Where's Baron?"

"Ahead of me. I don't know." Grofield's voice was husky and he was out of breath, but the words came as though he were fully conscious and in good shape. "I hid on the boat," he said. "Passed out. I don't know how far he is ahead of me."

Parker said, "How's he travelling? Light or heavy?"

"Heavy."

England said, "We'd better get this man back to the ship."

Grofield said, "No. I'm happy in Mexico."

Parker straightened up, said to England, "You got no jurisdiction here, remember?"

"This man's hurt," England said. "He needs medical attention."

On the ground, Grofield said, "Mexico has doctors."

Parker looked westward, across the flat land toward the horizon, and then he looked down at Grofield. He had too many things to do at once. It was no good leaving Grofield for the law, but it was also no good standing around here while Baron got farther and farther away.

He said to England, "We got a radio in that helicopter?"

"Of course."

"We got a map of this area in there?"

"I think so."

"Let's go look at it. You wait here, Grofield."

Grofield smiled some more, lying there on the ground. He looked very sick. "I won't move," he promised.

Parker and England went back to the helicopter and looked at a map. According to the pilot they were at a spot about twenty miles south of a coast town called Pesca. About fifteen miles west of them was a dirt road heading north and south, and that road, taken through a number of villages, would lead finally to Ciudad Victoria, about eighty miles away, the nearest city of any size.

Parker said to England, "You get on that radio of yours, you arrange for a jeep to come here from Ciudad Victoria. Then you and the helicopter leave. Grofield and I, in the jeep, we'll get Baron for you. Tell them we want to keep the jeep a while, maybe a few days, maybe a week. We'll turn it in when we go back across the border."

"I don't know if I can work that," England said. "You don't seem to realize how complicated that would be, getting—"

"Then why don't you try it, see what happens?"

England said, "I stay with you."

Parker looked at him. "You got no jurisdiction here."

"I won't be here officially. I'll just be with you, observing."

Parker shook his head. "No."

"It's the only way I could get a car, if it's checked out to me. They'd never allow me to give a car to you."

"Jeep."

"Jeep, yes. And I ride with you."

Parker thought a few seconds. This was wasting time, and he could see he wasn't getting anywhere. All right, he'd unload England when he had to. "Good," he said. "You come with us."

"I'll get on the radio right away, England said.

145

2

Grofield said, "Mother, in my last moments I was thinking of you."

Parker looked over at him, and Grofield was sitting up. They'd put him in the shade under the helicopter while waiting for the jeep, and now he was sitting up, holding to a strut with his right hand, smiling out at the world.

Parker went over to him and said, very low, so England wouldn't hear it, "Lie down, you moron. When that jeep gets here, I want you able to walk to it."

Grofield said, "Why?"

"Are you awake or asleep? Or maybe you think going to a hospital would be a good idea. If you're well enough to walk to the jeep we can justify you staying at a hotel. If we have to carry you, England will ship you to a hospital and there's nothing we can do about it, and from the hospital it's one step to the Mexican law, and they turn you over to our law, and I'll see you in fifteen, twenty years."

Grofield blinked. "Oh," he said. He lay down again, carefully. "I'm sorry, I'm not thinking. I'll be all right now."

"Good."

Around on the other side of the helicopter, England said, "Here it comes. Here comes the jeep."

Parker walked around and looked westward and saw the dust cloud. Beneath it something small and black was bouncing.

"At last," said England. He rubbed his hands together, like a man with lots to do. "Now we can get going."

England was a lot more chipper now, since he'd made the radio call and unloaded the responsibility. He no longer argued with Parker or stood around prophesying doublecrosses.

It took a long while for the jeep to come the last stretch; for a while it looked as though it were just bouncing up and down out there, not coming forward at all. But it finally showed up, braking heavily, and the Mexican driver jumped out with a toothy grin as the dust cloud caught up with the car, surrounded it, and dissipated. The driver walked out of the cloud, still grinning, slapping now at his trousers to get the dust off. He was stocky, mustachioed, swarthy, in civilian clothes: short-sleeved white shirt and dark gray slacks. He made a comic flourish and said, "Señores, your auto."

England was snapping his fingers, snapping his fingers. All of a sudden he was in a hurry. "Where's Grofield?" he said.

"Right here, never fear, right here." Grofield came around the helicopter, walking, smiling his nonchalance, his left hand tucked into his trouser pocket. "Just the day for a ride," he said.

"Sí, said the driver. "You know." He and Grofield seemed pleased by each other.

England got in front with the driver, and Parker and Grofield sat in back. Grofield had a little trouble getting in and Parker had to give him a boost, but once he was seated his smile flashed again and he said, "Ready as ever."

Parker slid into the seat beside him, and the jeep started around in a U-turn, heading back the way it had come. Behind them, the pilot was getting into his helicopter to take it back to its ship.

"Once around the park, driver," Grofield said. "I believe I'll take a nap." His smile got glassy and he passed out, his head falling over on Parker's shoulder.

Parker said, for England's benefit, "That's a good idea. Sleep the whole trip, why don't you?"

The first part of the trip, cross-country, was rough, and it was just as well Grofield had passed out at the beginning of it. The road, when they finally reached it and turned north on it, was good only by comparison.

They entered a village called Soto la Marina, a dirt street flanked by dirt houses. The main crop of this country seemed to be stones, so there were stone walls here and there.

After Soto la Marina they turned left on a road just like the first one. They were heading west again now, passing through a town called Casas that looked exactly the same as Soto la Marina except the road had begun to improve a little.

Just beyond Casas there were two men beside the road, an old one and a young one. The young one, big as a bull, was standing with his hands on his hips, watching the jeep go by. The old one, tired-looking, was sitting on an upended suitcase. The other suitcase was beside the young one's legs.

Parker didn't look back after the jeep went by.

They kept going, and a while later they passed through a town call Petaqueno. The road was getting better and better, and was blacktop by now. A sagging orange bus, wide as a whale, was taking passengers in the square, every passenger carrying a huge bundle wrapped in cloth.

Just beyond Petaqueno, Parker shifted Grofield's body so his weight went the other way, leaving Parker's left arm free. He poked around the floor and between the seats, because every jeep in the world has tools rattling around inside it, and he found a screwdriver and a wrench. He hefted the wrench, nodded, and said, "Stop for a second, will you?"

England turned around, frowning. "What for? We'll be in Victoria in fifteen minutes."

"This is an emergency. You, stop."

The driver smiled and shrugged and brought the jeep to a stop. "When you got to go," he said, and Parker hit England with the wrench. The driver made an O with his mouth and started to bring his arm up against the swinging wrench, but he was a little late.

Parker climbed out, lay Grofield across the back seats, pulled England and the driver out of the jeep onto the ground, got the .38 service revolver from England's pocket and put it in his own hip pocket, got behind the wheel of the jeep, and made a fast U-turn. He headed back for Casas.

3

They were walking along the road, toward Parker, and they didn't have the suitcases.

The dust cloud had told them, the trailing tan puff this jeep carried around behind itself on these roads like a comet's tail. They'd seen it coming, and they'd remembered the jeep that had gone by the other way a quarter of an hour before, and just in case there was a connection between jeep and dust cloud, between dust cloud and the man who once had carried those suitcases, just in case there was a connection they'd hidden the suitcases.

Near, very near. They were strolling along the road, and they couldn't have gone far from the road, so the suitcases were very near. Beyond them, the other side of them. They'd hidden the suitcases and started walking away from them, so that's where they had to be.

They looked straight ahead as they walked. Neither of them looked at Parker or the jeep at all.

Parker went on by them, and farther on another hundred yards, and then he stopped. He turned the jeep around and saw them standing still down there, the old man looking back and the young one tugging at his arm, trying to make him walk again. But then the young one saw it was too late, and let go the old man's arm, and the two of them watched.

Parker got out of the jeep. To his right, off the side of the road, there was a swath of dry brown ground, littered with pebbles, the swath about ten feet wide, ending at a low stone wall. The stone wall was about knee height, but fluctuated, and was made of the orange-brown stones that were lying all over this country, the stones of all different sizes, no cement used but just the stones piled up one on top of another, the low wall meandering along beside the road, separating dry brown lifeless ground from dry brown lifeless ground.

Parker walked along the road toward the two men, and then he turned around and walked back toward the jeep. He passed the jeep and walked another twenty yards, and then turned around and did it all over again.

On the second circuit he saw it, peeking up over the top of the wall, curved, plastic, black, alien.

The handle.

He let his lips spread in a smile. He started toward the handle.

As soon as he took a step away from the road, toward the wall, the two men began throwing stones at him. The old one had no arm, and the stones he threw were short, but the young one had a good arm and a good eye.

They were a nuisance, an irritation. Parker took England's revolver from his hip pocket and showed it to them. He didn't want to kill them, that was just stupid. There was no need for it.

But they kept throwing stones even after he showed them the gun, and now the old man was shouting, too: "Hi! Hi! Hi!"

Parker put a bullet in the dirt ahead of the young one's feet.

They both stopped. They looked at the ground where the puff had come up, and they looked at each other. They they both dropped the stones out of their hands.

But they wouldn't go away. They stood where they were, blankfaced, and they watched everything Parker did.

Parker walked the rest of the way over to the wall and bent slightly over it and put his hand around the protruding handle and lifted. The suitcase came up into view, satisfactorily full. He carried it back to the jeep and put it on the floor in front on the passenger's side. Then he went back to the wall and walked along it, looking over the tip, until he found the other suitcase. He picked that one up and carried it back, too.

On a hunch, he opened both suitcases. They were full of money, just as they were supposed to be, but the little flannel sacks of diamonds were gone.

He looked up, and the two of them were talking together, low-voiced but angry. One of them wanted to do one thing, and the other one wanted to do the other. Then they saw him looking at them, and they saw the suitcases open on the hood of the jeep, and they came to an agreement. Elaborately casual, watching Parker every inch of the way, they left the road, moved to the wall, clambered over it. The young one had to help the old one over the wall. When they were both over, they started walking. They walked straight out across country, away from the road.

Parker let them go. They weren't carrying the diamonds with them, or they'd still be in the suitcase, so they were probably buried somewhere near where Baron was buried. Parker spoke no Spanish, and it was unlikely either of those two spoke any English, so questioning them would be too complicated. There was enough in the suitcases anyway, and hanging around looking for the diamonds would take up too much time. For all those reasons, Parker let them go.

Way out there, they were walking faster and faster; now they were running. All in all, they were a comical pair.

Parker turned back to the jeep, and Grofield was sitting up, his face gray underneath the dirt. "Is that the geetus, love?" he asked.

"All but the diamonds." Parker shut the suitcases, put one on the floor in front and one on the floor in back. "We'll let the diamonds go," he said.

Grofield said, "Where oh where has my Baron gone?"

Parker pointed at the two dots running north along the rubbly ground. "I figure those two took care of him. They had the goods."

"England will be sad," Grofield said. He smiled, and looked around a little, and then frowned, saying, "Where is he? England, where is he?"

"We left him."

"You're a wonder, Parker."

Parker got behind the wheel. "Lay down," he said. "I can't drive this thing slow."

"I know you're doing the best you can, old man, but if you could fit a doctor in the schedule somewhere. . ."

"That's next," Parker told him. "Lay down."

"No sooner said." Smiling, Grofield lay down again, across the seats. When he closed his eyes, he looked dead.

151

4

Parker walked into American Express wih one hundred dollars
and walked out with one thousand two hundred fifty pesos.
Same difference.

Downstairs on the ground floor at American Express there
was a counter where people could have mail delivered, and a
steady stream of vacationing Americans passed by there,
looking for letters or money from home. There were young
schoolteachers on vacation, in groups of three and four, middle-
aged couples awkwardly overdressed in clothing too dark and
heavy for the climate, groups of shaggy young expatriates
looking exactly like their brothers and sisters in Greenwich
Village or the Latin Quarter of North Beach.

Parker hung around outside for about ten minutes, until a
shaggy loner went in looking hangdog and didn't get any mail at
the counter. He came out looking even sadder. His shoes were
unshined, his trousers were unpressed, his flannel shirt was
unwashed, his hair was uncut.

Parker said to him, "You. One minute."

"What? Me?"

"You speak Spanish?"

"Spanish? Sure. How come?"

"You want to make a fast ten?"

"Dollars?"

Everything this kid said was a question. Parker nodded.
"Dollars."

The kid grinned. "Who do I kill?"

"You come with me and you translate."

"Lead on."

"Come on, then," Parker said, and started down the street.
He was in Mexico City, on Avenue Niza. He led the way to

the corner, which was the Paseo de la Reforma, the main east-west street in Mexico City, and turned right. Reforma is a broad avenue, with grassy walks on both sides and statues at almost every major intersection.

Parker turned right on Reforma and walked down to the Avenue de Los Insurgentes, the main north-south street. At the intersection of Reforma and Insurgentes there was a regal statue of an Indian named Cuauhtemoc.

On Insurgentes, Parker flagged a *pesero*, a cab that would take him as far as he wanted to go on Insurgentes for one peso, or eight cents. *Peseros* worked both Insurgentes and Reforma, tearing back and forth in red or orange Chevies and Opels and Taunuses, carrying from one to five passengers.

There were already three passengers in the back of this cab, so Parker and the kid got in front with the driver, and they went shooting north.

Parker and the kid were the last passengers off, up at Avenue Paganini near the city limits. Parker had to break a ten peso note, and the cabby made change in a hurry; he wanted to turn around and race south again. As soon as Parker had his eight pesos and was out of the cab, the driver tore away.

"This way," said Parker, and walked down Avenue Paganini, passing the jeep where he'd left it for good.

Mexico City was five hundred miles farther from the American border than Casas, but it made sense to come here and so Parker had come. England and the rest of his crowd would be looking hard for Parker now, but they'd be looking in all the wrong places. Up at the border and down around Ciudad Victoria, depending whether they thought he was trying to break away to find Baron. So the thing to do was stay away from Ciudad Victoria and stay away from the border.

And the other thing to do, until he could get out of Meixco completely, was go where Americans were the least noticeable, and that was Mexico City. So when he'd left Casas with the suitcases he'd retraced the original route back through Soto la Marina and south from there past where they'd picked up the road in the first place when they'd come inland from the sea, and from there on down to Aldama, where there was a government station selling Pemex gas, the only brand available in Mexico. They didn't have any Fasolmex, the premium grade, so Parker had them fill the jeep and the spare five-gallon can with Supermexolina, the cheaper grade. With luck this would carry him all the way to Mexico City, and he wouldn't have to make any more stops along the way, leave any more signs of his trail.

Below Aldama the road improved. He continued south to Manuel, the west to Ciudad Mante, a fair-sized town full of men and boys but short on visible women, where he picked up route 85, a main north-south route that took him straight into Mexico City. They slept on the road above Zimapan Monday night, and got into Mexico City a little before noon on Tuesday, and Parker was no sooner across the city line than he found a doctor for Grofield and he ditched the jeep.

He'd decided Grofield could wait for a doctor, rather than waste time on the road before they could get rid of the jeep. Grofield's wound wasn't bleeding, and he was unconscious most of the time, so he was no trouble to transport. Every now and then he'd wake up, do some of his comic routines, and then fade away again.

Now, with Grofield at the doctor's, with pesos in his pocket, with a good Spanish-speaking guide who looked too naive to do anything but keep his mouth shut, Parker felt he had breathing room again. He walked down Avenue Paganini and when he got to the doctor's house he said to the kid, "Don't ask any questions. Don't say anything at all. You're a clam."

The kid nodded. "I'm a clam," he said. He no longer looked hangdog; excitement and curiosity danced in his eyes.

Parker went into the doctor's house, a white stucco building behind a white stucco wall with a black metal gate in it. The gate was open now, but at night it would be locked. Glass shards were embedded in the top of the wall. The gap between the haves and the have-nots was wider here than in the States, which made the haves a lot warier.

Inside, the doctor was coldly indignant. "This man," he said, "should have been to a doctor two days ago. He should be in a hospital. I don't care how severe he thinks his marital problems are, his medical problems believe me are much worse." He was a short, slender, olive-skinned man with a thin mustache, large outraged eyes, and perfect accent-free English.

Parker had given him a song and dance about Grofield being a husband caught in bed with another man's wife, being shot by husband number two, being terrified that his own wife would find out about it because she was the one in the family with money. It was a story of intrigue, romance, danger, and derring-do that he and Grofield had worked out beforehand, the kind of story Grofield could act with a lot of gusto and the doctor could take a Latin pleasure in.

But now the doctor was indignant, outraged. "*He* seems to have no comprehension of the severity of his wound," he said, motioning angrily at the closed door behind which lay Grofield, "but you're his friend, you should have forced him to come here before this."

"There wasn't anything I could do, Doctor. He's got a mind of his own."

Then it went on like that for a while, the doctor talking out his sense of outrage, Parker being as patient with him as he could, the kid watching with bright-eyed lack of comprehension.

Finally the doctor was done. Parker had had to let him run out his string, so there wouldn't be any trouble later on, but he was glad when it was finally done. "I'll see he takes care of himself from now on," he said. "Can I take him with me now?"

"He's a very sick man."

"I know that."

"I've removed the bullet and bandaged the wound, and I've given him a sedative. He's asleep."

"What does that mean?"

The doctor said, "It means he's asleep. He should be allowed to rest."

155

"That's all right with you, if he sleeps here awhile?"

"Of course."

Parker looked at his watch. "What if I come back at six o'clock?"

"Very well."

"Good. You want me to pay you now or then?"

"Then. It doesn't matter."

"I'll take my bags now."

"All right. They're in the corner there, where you left them."

Parker had told him the suitcases were his, but had offered no explanation. People don't explain themselves to one another when they're on the up-and-up; let the doctor work up his own theory about the suitcases.

Now, Parker took them and motioned to the kid to come on, and they left the doctor's house and went back out to the street. The kid said, "You want me to carry one of those?"

"Sure. Why not?"

They walked back up to Insurgentes, each carrying a suitcase. They had to wait awhile for a *pesero*, because not many of them came out this far.

While they were waiting, Parker said, "What I want now is a hotel. Not a Hilton, but not a dive. A small quiet hotel where they mind their own business. Away from the centre of town, if possible."

"Most of the big tourist hotels are around the Alameda," the kid said. "You want to be away from them?"

"Right."

"Then there's some others right off Insurgentes, down near Reforma. Back in around the *jai alai frontón*. Small, but they speak English, most of them."

"That's what we want. You lead the way."

A *pesero* family came and they rode it back toward the middle of town, getting off at Avenue Gomes Farias, heading east toward the Plaza de la Republica. They tried two hotels but both were full, and finally found one behind the *frontón* on Edison.

156

"The room isn't for me," Parker explained. "I'm getting it for a friend of mine. This is his luggage."

"So you sign his name," said the clerk. He spoke English with a combination of Greenpoint and Mexican accents.

Parker wrote "Joseph Goldberg, New York City," and the clerk himself took them up in the elevator to the room, carrying the two suitcases. Parker gave him a five-peso note, stashed the suitcases in the closet, and said to the kid, "Now we do some buying."

For the next hour and a half they went from store to store, while Parker bought clothing and other stuff. He got two suits, four white shirts, two belts, five ties, two pairs of shoes and six of socks, five sets of underwear, a raincoat, a toothbrush and tube of toothpaste, a hairbrush, a razor and a packet of blades, a can of shoe polish, two Mexican guidebooks and an English-Spanish dictionary, two cheap silver bracelets gift-wrapped, two quarts of tequila, a straw ladies' handbag, an expensive leather suitcase, a small original oil painting in a wooden frame all about a foot square, an high-priced carton of American cigarettes, a Zippo lighter, and a can of lighter fluid. The kid guided him from place to place, translated when necessary, and toted the goods.

Back at the hotel, with the boxes and bags of stuff all spread out on the bed, Parker took a ten-dollar bill from his wallet and said, "You been a big help. I'm done now."

"It was a pleasure," the kid said. "Trying to figure out what the hell you're doing, it's better than the puzzle in the Sunday *Times*."

Parker gave him the ten and said, "You here on a tourist visa or a passport?"

"Tourist visa."

"You want to make some more dough?"

The kid grinned. "You know it."

"Fifty bucks," Parker said.

"Fifty? What do I do this time?"

"Lose your wallet."

The kid blinked. "What?"

"Lose your wallet, before you leave this room. Tomorrow you go to the American Embassy, you tell them somebody stole your wallet with all your papers in it. You do that tomorrow afternoon, not before then."

"Mister, I could get in a lot of trouble do—"

"For losing your wallet? Red tape, that's all. It happens all the time."

The kid took his wallet out and looked at it. "You don't need the wallet, do you? Just the papers."

"I'll make it sixty," Parker told him, "you can buy a new wallet."

"I've got pictures in—"

"Get new copies. If the wallet is lost it's lost."

"Oh. Yeah, I guess so." The kid hefted the wallet. "I sure wish I knew what was going on."

"I'm a counterspy," Parker told him. "I got to get to Washington before the Russkis start World War Three."

"It's something like that," the kid said. He took his new ten-dollar bill and a few pesos from the wallet and tossed it on the bed. "How do you like that?" he said. "I lost my wallet."

"You report it not before tomorrow afternoon."

"Got it."

Parker fed him sixty dollars, in tens, and the kid went away.

For the next few hours Parker was very busy. He took the suitcases out of the closet and opened them on the bed and started counting, and when he got to one hundred and twenty-seven thousand, five hundred sixty, he was finished. That was sixty-three thousand, seven hundred eighty dollars apiece. Not the two hundred grand Karns had guaranteed him, but he wouldn't bother about hitting Karns for the rest. The diamonds would have covered that much, probably, and even so his half was more than the fifty thousand dollars his quarter would originally have been.

He put Grofield's share back in one of the suitcases and stowed that one in the closet. Then he phoned the airport and booked passage on an eight-thirty flight that evening to Los Angeles, and after that he packed.

The packing took a long while. He had two suitcases, the old one and one he'd just bought, and all his new purchases. The clothing he'd been wearing went in first, and he put on all fresh things, and after that he worked slowly.

He had a large mass of money, and what he had to do was break it into a lot of small masses of money and make those small masses of money disappear. There were bills rolled in the new socks, each sock around a little stack of money large enough to make one rolled sock look like two. He tucked bills in the toes of the spare shoes, and filled all pockets of the suits. The new shirts, with the wrapping taken off, looked as though they'd just come back from the cleaners, and into each he stuffed more bills. Each piece of underwear was rolled up with a chunk of money inside it like a pearl in an oyster. The ladies' handbag was crammed with bills. The raincoat pockets were filled with bills and the clothing Parker was wearing was packed full of bills. It took work and it took time, but when he was done the cash was all packed away and out of sight. With the painting, the handbag, the bottles of tequila and all the other stuff, he looked exactly like a tourist, and obvious tourists get a quick runthrough at customs.

At six o'clock he went back to the doctor's house, paid the tab, and picked up Grofield. Grofield was conscious and shaky, but grinning. He looked a mess in his clothes, but that couldn't be helped.

They took a *pesero* back downtown, and walked the three blocks to the hotel. "That was a good man," Grofield said. "That doctor."

"He did a good job on you."

"I'm not ready to travel yet, though. Not yet."

"I know." Parker nodded. "That's your hotel, ahead. You're Joseph Goldberg there."

"Who are you?"

"Nobody."

Parker didn't explain any more till they were up in the room, where Grofield immediately stretched out on the bed, saying, "I'm weak as a kitten, you know that?"

"You're checked in here alone," Parker told him. "I'm leaving tonight. Your share's in the suitcase in the closet. They'll be looking for us together, so the sooner we split the better."

Grofield nodded. "Sure."

"Sooner or later they'll find the jeep and know we came down here, so play it tight."

"I will."

Parker looked around. "That's all of it," he said. He picked up the suitcases, was carrying the raincoat tucked under his left arm. "I'll be seeing you," he said.

Grofield said, "I appreciate this."

"Appreciate what?"

"You didn't leave me up there. You carried me along, got me my share."

Parker didn't understand what there was to appreciate about that. "We were working together," he said.

"That's right," Grofield said. "I'll be seeing you."